"K.P. Yohannan calls for all-out, no-holds-barred commitment to follow Christ. In a world of compromise we need his challenge."

Dr. Robert Coleman
Author of *Master Plan of Evangelism*

"India has produced heroes esteemed by this world. Their names have become synonymous with peaceful protest or with religious self-sacrifice. K.P. Yohannan, however, stands for a cause, which the world doesn't applaud. The world can't see his steadfast protest against the adversary of God or his endless self-sacrifice to deliver the Bread of Life to dying humanity. K.P. lives only for the applause of Heaven.

"There is something about this unobtrusive man that makes you want to fight alongside him. He may not be a towering giant in the world's estimation, but he is a mighty force for the Kingdom of God. In *Against the Wind,* K.P. Yohannan *inspires* self-sacrifice. He makes you want to row against the winds of wickedness in a world of compromise."

Ray Comfort
Founder of Living Waters Publication, Author and Speaker

"*Against the Wind* is a book I've waited a lifetime to see written by someone who truly lives such a message. There is simply no challenge that is more important right now for both pastors in the pulpit or people in the pew than K.P. Yohannan's timely guide to finishing well in a world of compromise. Every Christian leader and layworker in the church globally needs this message."

Dr. Dick Eastman
International President of Every Home for Christ

"In the age of counterfeit Christianity, false gospels, and false teachers, thank the Lord that K.P. has spoken to the issue. When you read this book and apply the godly commands, you will be able to look in the mirror and see a better reflection of Christ. Even 'against the wind' we can go forward in the power of Christ."

William Fay
Author of *Share Jesus without Fear*

"*Against the Wind* has an important message. As results and marketing strategies powerfully invade the church today, there is little incentive left to guard our personal lives. The result: Many people with so much potential end up disillusioned and disheartened. This book provides the needed correction to this spiritual epidemic."

Dr. Ajith Fernando
Author and National Director of Youth for Christ, Sri Lanka

"Dr. K.P. Yohannan has challenged us to stand firm in this world of compromise. He has reminded us once again how relevant God's Word is to both life and ministry. The emphasis on integrity, holiness, servanthood, grace and finishing well are sorely needed by those who are answering the call to be the Lord's servants. This is what I call a 'Selah' book. It should be read a chapter at a time, taking time to reflect and meditate, then prayerfully determine what God has for you in the reading."

Dick Hugoniot
President of Wycliffe Bible Translators International

"Being a busy person, when I received the manuscript for *Against the Wind* in the mail, I scheduled a couple hours to speed-read the manuscript so I could offer this endorsement. I was unexpectedly, however, stopped in my tracks by the truth and passion in which K.P. attacks the growing monster of Compromise in the body of Christ. I found *Against the Wind* to be written both with the fatherly instruction and scholarly concern of a John Stott or Chuck Smith, but also with the biting prophetic edge of a Tozer or Keith Green.

"I will be ordering *Against the Wind* by the case to distribute to our YWAM missionaries to help guard them against compromise, as well as to my pastor/evangelist friends who need the same words and warnings. My prayer is that *Against the Wind* would have wide acceptance in the body of Christ. It is a message that is urgently needed."

Danny Lehmann
Director of YWAM Hawaii and Author

"If tender pats and soothing words are what you want because serving Christ has proven a bit tougher than what you anticipated, this book is not for you. But if you're ready for a word from the Lord delivered by a seasoned leader who knows what it takes for ministry to be effective, then you've found what you've been looking for."

Dr. David R. Mains
Executive Director of Mainstay Ministries

"Drawn from his own life experience on the mission field, K.P. Yohannan writes as one who has been on both sides of the mentoring spectrum. This veteran leader has been molded by other great leaders and has himself shaped the lives of scores of others. This is the same pattern that the Apostle Paul used with young Timothy and other first-century leaders like him. In this book K.P. borrows from that relationship and then reflects on his own lifetime of experiences to create a rich and invaluable resource for running and finishing our lives well. I have always enjoyed K.P. Yohannan as a friend as well as an author. I resonate with his practical straightforward style. After thirty-plus years of running well, K.P. shows us that the real issue is ending up as well as we began."

Pastor Skip Heitzig
Senior Pastor of Ocean Hills Church and Author of *When God Prays*

"With characteristic depth and thoroughness, K.P. Yohannan has tackled a topic that faces all of us, or will. The principles he covers are those that need continual honing, whether our walk has been seasoned with years or yet only months. K.P. has the mind of ten men, the heart of a hundred—yet with a humility that is the true test of a man of God. The points are practical, the tenor inspirational, the conviction motivational. In the end, it all comes down to the individual—each one of us—what we're going to do, and the depth of our passions. The food served here is not milk, but true meat."

Hyatt Moore
Author, Artist, Former President of Wycliffe Bible Translators, USA

against the wind

FINISHING WELL
IN A WORLD
OF COMPROMISE

K.P. YOHANNAN

BOOKS

a division of Gospel for Asia

www.gfa.org

ISBN: 1–59589–047–5 (softcover)

Published by gfa books, a division of Gospel for Asia
1800 Golden Trail Court, Carrollton, TX 75010
phone: (972) 300-7777
fax: (972) 300-7778

Printed in the United States of America

For more information about other materials, visit our website: www.gfa.org.

dedication

I dedicate this book to my leaders scattered throughout
10 Asian nations, Europe and North America. Thank you for
taking up the challenge to serve our Lord with commitment
and all diligence. I am grateful for the price that you daily
choose to pay, often quietly and unnoticed.

Continue on with the fervor in which you have started,
and our Lord will tell you on that day, *Well done, My good and
faithful servant. Enter into My rest.*

contents

preface

The content of this book is taken from a series I taught in January 2001 to more than 500 brothers and sisters at the Gospel for Asia Field Leaders Conference in India. The many letters, emails and telephone calls I received, testifying of the transformation the Lord brought into their lives as a result of this teaching, encourage me that the Lord, in His mercy, will do the same for you.

Because this series was intended for the leaders of our ministry, our thought was to release this material in print for the additional 14,500 pastors and evangelists who serve with us in 10 Asian nations. Then, as I began to read the feedback from those who attended the meeting, I felt strongly the need to have it available for a wider circulation in the Body of Christ at large. Hence, this edition.

For simplicity and clarity, the spoken form and original audience have been maintained. My hope is that the reader will hear the message with his heart as he reads it. My desire and prayer are that the message of this book will help you draw nearer to Christ, to learn His ways and stay true to Him until the very end.

Timothy listened well to Paul's instruction, and history testifies of the incredible effectiveness he had in his life and ministry. In this study on the characteristics that help the man of God grow in character and fulfill the call of God, I pray that the Lord would give you understanding of how to translate them for your own life, whether in full-time ministry, a student, a businessman or a simple mother.

May you be one who remains true to Christ and His call in a world of compromise, and may the Lord bless you.

acknowledgments

As with any book, there are many people who played a part in producing and making this book what it is today. I am grateful to each one of you.

The content of this book was taken from 21 hours of teaching for our leaders in India. Thank you, Natalie Schulz, for transcribing all of these tapes so quickly. Nicole Nichols, thank you for your diligence in working through the manuscript. Your insight and reliance on the Lord for His help are integral parts of how this book came out. I am grateful. And thank you, Teresa Chupp and Kim Smith, for your overall coordination of this project. I appreciate your help.

Finally, I want to thank my wife, Gisela, for all these years of standing with me in serving the Lord. During the many times when the wind seemed to beat against us so strong, you stood by my side with such faithfulness to our Lord. Words cannot tell you how grateful I am. I love you.

introduction

In a telephone conversation some years ago, I asked George Verwer, the founder of Operation Mobilization and a dear friend of mine, "George, how is everything going?"

He responded, "Blessings come with buffeting."

How true that statement is. Within our own ministry, we see how on one hand the work is growing at an incredible rate and the Lord is doing tremendous things among us. Yet trials, failures, setbacks and persecutions are present as well.

This pattern is also very similar to that of the early Church. Scarcely 30 years after Pentecost, the Church was confronting such struggles from within and from without that Paul, writing in Philippians 2:21, reported that Timothy was the only one of his coworkers left! Everyone else sought their own. If it was not money they sought, it was position. If not position, then some kind of approval or hidden agenda.

Who were these people who once served with Paul but now had turned away? Surprisingly, they were supposed to have been the best of the best, those who were thought to have been absolutely committed to Christ and His call. What, then, went wrong?

The reason I ask this question is because the Church is in a much similar situation today, dealing with the same issues of compromise among believers and leaders in the ministry.

A study done on corporate rise and decline indicated that the freshness and spontaneous growth of an organization last about 25 years. After that it plateaus, then declines.

The movement of Gospel for Asia is now 25 years old. We are scattered in 10 Asian nations with more than 14,500 pastors, missionaries and evangelists preaching the Gospel. There are more than 54 Bible colleges and 9,500 Believers Churches and 12,000 mission stations spread out all over the Subcontinent. As we move ahead with the ministry, I am deeply concerned about the future of the work, knowing that the eternal destiny of millions of souls is at stake.

What is the answer to my concern? What will keep us on course and lead us on, enabling us to say like Paul, "I have fought the good fight, I have finished the race, I have kept the faith" (2 Timothy 4:7)? It is this one thing: the character of the servants of the Lord—every missionary on the field, every teacher in the Bible colleges, every mother and father raising their children, all the regional and state leaders appointed over the work. Only godly character within will sustain us and keep us on track, both individually and as a movement, to fulfill the purpose for which the Lord has called us.

Yet as was the case with the early Church, as time goes by, the character and deep, true devotion that should mark the servant of God often becomes the exception rather than the rule. A movement that may have started with 500 people, 90 percent of whom were true, passionate and serious about following Christ and His commands, slowly declines to 50 percent, then 40, then 30, until finally the faithful and true are the minority.

Take a look at the history of many well-known ministries, and you will find this to be true. So many church denominations that started out with such great fervor and zeal have fallen by the wayside, often because of this one thing: The character of its workers turns from godliness to corruption, as they become lovers of money, power and position. Their hearts grow cold, their passion is diluted and the ministry becomes so distorted that God Himself exclaims, "Ichabod!"—the glory has departed! Oh, how I pray that we as a ministry and you individually do not follow this course!

In every generation, God has His remnant—people who are willing to obey His call and pour out their lives to do His work. May you and I be those whose hearts continue to burn for Christ, always pressing on toward the mark! My prayer is such that God will find among us another Martin Luther, a Bakht Singh, an Amy Carmichael or a Pandita Ramabai. God is looking for one more young man like John Knox of Scotland, who did not pray, "Give me money, future, position, education," but rather, "O God, give me my nation or I will die!"

Are we like that? Can we pray those prayers? Can we count the cost and give up our own ambitions to follow our Savior on the narrow road He has marked out for us? O God, make us able! Only as we are refined within, conformed to the image—*the character*—of Christ, will we be able to run this way and reach the finish line.

The apostle Paul knew well the importance of character in the life of the believer. That is why in his last letter he instructs Timothy through 19 specific characteristics, which I will highlight in this book. Each is a crucial element that must be present in our lives if we are to finish well the race we started.

We have God's promise that as we listen and obey His ways, we will keep on the right course and, like Paul, run the race and keep the faith, fulfilling the purposes of God in our generation.

a higher call

One person.

It only takes one person to rout the forces of darkness and establish a testimony for the glory of God.

History bears witness to this truth as it reminds us of *individuals*—Martin Luther, Pandita Ramabai, Sadhu Sundar Singh, Moses, Elijah. The list could go on and on. In every generation, there are the individuals who *chose* to rise above the easy norm, set their face like flint and thus accomplish great things for God.

From the beginning of time, God has sought for these kinds of individuals, those to whom He can show Himself strong and through whom He can bring about His plans and purposes on earth. Consider what 2 Chronicles 16:9 (NLT) tells us—"The eyes of the LORD search the whole earth in order to strengthen those whose hearts are fully committed to him."

But God doesn't always find the people He is looking for. We see the truth of this in His lament in Ezekiel 22:30 (NASB), "I searched for a man among them who would build up the wall and stand in the gap before Me for the land, so that I would not destroy it; *but I found no one*" (emphasis mine). Read a few paragraphs before this verse, and you will find that God was searching among those called by His name—His prophets, leaders and priests.

If God were searching among us today, would He find in you the kind of person He is looking for?

Well, God *is* searching among us today, searching for the one among His people who will make the choice to seek Him and conform his life to His principles, following Him regardless of what kind of compromise or complacency may surround. God is not looking for the majority who claim to be His, but for those authentic few, who, by their character, demonstrate that they are His and that they follow Him above all else. Unfortunately, I fear that many within the Body of Christ may be passed by in His search for men and women like this.

I realize this is a strong statement, but that is just what we need to wake us from our slumber and spiritual lethargy.

Satan has done a masterful job of deception within the Body of Christ. Christianity has been redefined to fit modern society. It is now a good moneymaking business. The Christian music and entertainment industry skyrockets, while the Word of God is peddled for profit and the authentic Christian life of surrender and obedience is tossed aside as legalism. More than 2 billion people who do not know Jesus head toward hell to perish for eternity, while the Church laughs its way to hysteria, claiming this is the sign of the last days' outpouring of the Holy Spirit. Instead of laying down our lives to serve the purposes of God, we try numerous ways to make the Almighty God our servant to fulfill all our dreams and desires. My brothers and sisters, this is not Christianity.

A.W. Tozer, a 20th-century prophet who knew God intimately and spoke fearlessly to his generation, says it perfectly—"That this world is a playground instead of a battleground has now been accepted in practice by the vast majority of fundamentalist Christians. They are facing both ways, enjoying Christ and the world too."[1] The Church has fallen headlong into carnality, and unless a true revival of repentance takes place, we are heading toward another "dark ages."

Warning of the apostasy and carnality that would come upon the Church, Tozer writes,

> Christianity is so entangled with the world that millions never guess how radically they have missed the New Testament pattern. Compromise is everywhere. The world is whitewashed just enough to pass inspection by blind men posing as believers. . . .
>
> Evangelical Christianity is now tragically below the New Testament standard. Worldliness is an accepted part of our way of life. Our religious mood is social instead of spiritual. We have lost the art of worship. We are not producing saints. Our models are successful business men, celebrated athletes and theatrical personalities. We carry on our religious activities after the methods of the modern advertiser. Our homes have been turned into theatres. Our literature is shallow and our hymnody borders on sacrilege. And scarcely anyone appears to care.
>
> Much that passes for New Testament Christianity is little more than objective truth sweetened with song and made palatable by religious entertainment.[2]

How true these words are. We indeed have gone this route, and something must change. We have settled, content with the fact that we have at least started the race. We have forgotten what Scripture makes clear—it is not how we started the race, but how we run and how we finish. "As Christ's soldier, do not let yourself become tied up in the affairs of this life, for then you cannot satisfy the one who has enlisted you in his army. Follow the Lord's rules for doing his work, just as an athlete either follows the rules or is disqualified and wins no prize" (2 Timothy 2:4–5, NLT).

I wonder how many in the Church today would be disqualified in the end. It is a sobering thought.

This was Paul's same concern for the Church in his day. In his years of ministry, Paul had seen an element of digression in the Body of Christ. That is the reason his epistles address a wide variety of sins, all that had crept into the churches over time. He had seen many fall away, as well as many who physically stayed a part of the Church but in their hearts and their actions were far from God. Soon Paul would no longer be around to address these issues and bring the necessary correction and encouragement, keeping the churches on course. This task is the one to which God had called Timothy.

So Paul, having pressed on for 30 relentless years to fulfill the call of God, now sits in his last prison cell, awaiting his death. Looking back over the years and knowing the seriousness of the task to which God has called his son in the faith, Paul sets out to leave Timothy with a guidebook on how to fulfill the ministry.

However, the essence of Paul's message did not focus on particular topics as much as it did on this one sole element— Timothy's *character*. You see, Paul knew that good infrastructure was not what was needed to ensure the growth and stability of the Church in the years to come, nor was it any external element. It is upon *character* that people and movements either rise or fall. If Timothy's character was solid and true, all else would fall into place, and Timothy would finish well the race the Lord Jesus had called him to run.

It is interesting how Paul communicates this message to Timothy. As John Stott points out in his book *Guard the Gospel*, "There are three little words he uses four times throughout this small book that crystallize the heart of his message to Timothy.

Translated from the Greek *su de,* meaning 'But for you . . .' (see 2 Timothy 2:1; 3:10, 14; 4:5)."[3]

"Timothy, within the Church there will be a decline in godliness. People are going to be arrogant and lovers of money. They will be greedy. They will not be submissive, but rebellious. False teachers will rise up. *But for you . . .*

"There will be carnal reasoning among believers, backsliding, laziness, self-centered living and self-seeking. But for you, Timothy, be different! Be bold as a lion; don't be afraid. Be authentic and genuine. Be unselfish. Don't follow the crowd. If need be, Timothy, stand alone. *But for you,* be faithful until the end. There is a crown waiting for you."

This call to live by godly character is the same message we in this world of compromise and casual Christianity need to hear today. That is why I bring Paul's words to remembrance and say: My brothers and sisters, *but for you,* be different. It is only the one "who overcomes and does [His] will to the end" (Revelation 2:26) who will receive the reward. Full-time Christian workers all around us may grow cold and their love for Christ may fade. Many will pursue money, honor from men, position and power, and will seek their own. *But for you,* stay on the narrow road. Walk alone if need be. Always remember there is a higher call.

A few years ago, I heard of one brother from Tripura who remembered this higher call and pursued the narrow road. By the grace of God, he planted seven churches in three months' time. When asked his secret to such success, he replied, "I pray as much as I work and work as much as I pray." This small statement gave a glimpse into the solid, godly character within this man.

It was not merely his actions that made me remember him or that made the difference in his ministry. Most anyone can discipline themselves to perform all the right actions. What matters is where these actions flow from. And for this man, it was a heart that was committed to Jesus. Like Paul, he sought to be well-pleasing to God and run strong the race He had set before him.

It is this kind of life and character that makes the difference. If you were to ask this brother, "How much does your church pay you for working five hours and praying five more? How much do they pay you for being like your Master, who stayed up all night to pray?" He would surely reply, "What did you say? What do you mean, 'How much do I get paid for praying during the night?' "

You see, this question has no meaning for him. His life is hidden in Christ, and he lives for Him alone, not for recognition, not for a salary and not for personal gain. He serves and lives by godly character, knowing that it was God who called him and it is God alone whom he must please.

We are at a crossroads, individually and as a ministry also. The Lord has entrusted to us the task of reaching millions with the Good News. Let us then have ears to hear the plea of the Holy Spirit through Paul's words to live differently, guard what has been entrusted to us, work hard, teach others, endure hardship, stay pure, remain faithful and fulfill the ministry. In essence, we must be men and women of godly character, who, in the midst of much compromise, choose to stay true to Christ and His call and thus fulfill the purpose for which He has called us.

As I close my eyes and try to feel the heartbeat of Paul, I can almost hear him say, "Timothy, follow my example, son. I did not give up, no matter how much hunger, nakedness, beatings, shipwreck, imprisonment, rejection and misunderstanding I faced. Compromise may surround you. This journey will be an uphill climb. *But for you*—you stay on course. The wind that will blow against your face may be bitter cold and fierce. Your Lord faced that same wind against Him—don't expect any less as you follow Him."

This kind of living is a choice that only you can make. Only you can choose to press on. God's grace will meet you at the point of your decision. When others around you, even those you may have once esteemed, look for an easier, more relaxed road, only you can make the choice to press past that and continue your pursuit, pressing on toward the mark. No matter what others may be doing or what may be accepted as the norm, hear the Lord Jesus saying, *But for you, you follow Me. Set your hand to the plow, and My grace will be there to keep you, if only you choose to stand against the wind and press on toward the higher call.*

I invite you, then, to come with me as we sit beside Timothy and meditate on Paul's final instructions. What does it mean and what does it look like to live out this kind of commitment to the very end? You have been called by God for a very specific purpose. What does it take to fulfill that purpose and bring honor to His name?

I pray that through each of these 19 characteristics, you would take the time to allow the Lord to penetrate your heart and give you the understanding of how to translate them into your own life. By keeping your heart open to His searching and applying His truth, you stay on the steady course to fulfill the call of God no matter what. May you be given strength to run strong in His grace and join in the great line of men and women who set their faces like flint and accomplished great things for God. Will you be one to stand out from the rest and be remembered in heaven and on earth for the impact you made upon your generation? Will you choose to stand against the wind and be recognized by God in His search for men?

The choice is yours.

called by God

There is great significance in the way Paul introduces himself at the start of 2 Timothy: "an apostle of Christ Jesus *by the will of God."*

From the first letter he wrote to this his last, Paul knew this one thing: He was called by God. It was not man who called him, it was not the need that drove him, nor was it anything from or for himself. He is making this fact clear to Timothy, saying, "I want you to know that I have not been running this race for 30 years because I wanted to do it. I haven't been doing it because Barnabas called me or because a church paid me. I am not in this because my parents said, 'He will be a servant of God' or because of some organization or Bible college. My ministry is by *His* will. I am doing this for one reason: God called me" (see Acts 13:1–2).

In 2 Timothy 1:9 and 11, Paul presses his point further, saying that it is God "who has saved us and called us" and who has appointed him as "a herald and an apostle and a teacher."

Paul's reason for making this so clear is because the assurance of your call is the foundational element to staying in the race for the long haul. This knowledge acts as a stronghold to fall back on when the going gets tough. And when the end seems so far out of sight, it is this calling from the Holy One that propels you forward one more step. Everything in your behavior and attitude is influenced, guided and regulated by this one factor.

Although the call of God that we are addressing now refers to the full-time call to ministry, please understand that each and every one of us is called by God for His purposes. As His daughters and sons, inheritors of the kingdom, each one of us is called to live as witnesses to His great power, love and salvation. Vocation does not change this fact. We will all give account of how we have fulfilled the requirement—the privilege—of bearing witness to Him in our generation.

Knowing You Are Called

There is a distinct call into full-time ministry, and it is this call that both Paul and Timothy heard, along with many others who had gone before them. All throughout the Bible, we see those who were called by God for specific purposes. In Exodus 3–4:17, we see how Moses did not appoint himself to lead the children of Israel; the Lord called him.

The prophet Amos is another example. He was just a simple farmer, with no one in his family ever having served the Lord. When those God sent him to questioned what he was doing, he defended himself, saying, "I was no prophet, nor was I a son of a prophet, but I was a sheepbreeder and a tender of sycamore fruit. Then the LORD took me as I followed the flock, and the LORD said to me, 'Go, prophesy to My people Israel' " (Amos 7:14–15, NKJV). He knew God had called him for that ministry.

And, of course, Jesus called His disciples. In Mark 3:14 we are told that "He appointed twelve—designating them apostles—that they might be with him and that he might send them out to preach."

On and on, from Moses, Isaiah, Jeremiah, Jonah and Paul, we see how those in the ministry are those whom God has called.

However, in the kingdom of God today, there are many ministries and organizations with hundreds of staff members seeing that the work is done. But there is a definite difference between a profession and a call:

A job, a profession, is one you choose; a ministry is one Christ chooses for you.

A job depends on your abilities; a ministry depends on your availability to God.

In a job you expect to receive something—a salary; in a ministry you expect to give.

A job well done brings you self-esteem; a ministry well done brings honor to Jesus Christ.

In a job you give something to get something; in a ministry you return something that has already been given to you.

A job well done has a temporal reward; a ministry well done has eternal rewards.[1]

I want to ask you: Are you called? Have you heard the Lord Jesus call you, saying, "Come, follow Me, be with Me and I will send you out for ministry"? The person you become, the decisions you make, the manner in which you behave and your attitude toward the Lord's work all depend on this deep conviction that you have been called by God.

Qualified by the Call

When we know we have been called by God, we can have the assurance that, no matter what we may experience or the weaknesses we see in ourselves, He will equip us with everything we need to fulfill that call.

The youthful Timothy was one called by the Lord, even though Scripture reveals that by the world's standards he did not seem like an adequate candidate to take on the responsibility of the ministry. Timothy was a young man, weak in body and shy by nature—not exactly the qualities we would particularly look for in one who was to take the place of the great apostle Paul.

One of the verses that reveals this is 1 Timothy 4:12, in which Paul encourages Timothy to not "let anyone look down on you because you are young." Paul was aware that Timothy might feel inadequate for the ministry because of his age and lack of experience. But nonetheless, God had called Timothy to this task. The knowledge of his calling must be enough for him to rise up and take heart.

You, too, may feel inadequate for the job you have been given. You may struggle just to maintain even the image of someone called by God. When the Lord called me, I was just 16 years old. When I first became a team leader, I was barely 19. If God could use me—fragile, weak and insecure—to lead others in the ministry, there is hope for every young person called by God, no matter what they lack.

If you feel discouraged because of a lack of experience or other things, please remember that if you know you are inexperienced, you are in good shape. Only when you think you are able and mature and can succeed on your own are you really in trouble. God gives grace to those who are weak and humble, using them in the mightiest of ways. But He opposes the proud who think they have it all together and can do the work on their own.

Not only was Timothy young, but he was also prone to illness. He lived continually with the problem of physical infirmity. We know this because Paul said to him in 1 Timothy 5:23, "Stop drinking only water, and use a little wine because of your stomach and your frequent illnesses."

You, too, may be living with physical deficiencies. Are you called to do something huge and significant but feel like saying, "My God, I am not able to handle it; I am tired and sick"? Well, Timothy was like that, and Paul encouraged him to press on to do the job God called him to do despite his illnesses.

Add to his young age and constant illnesses, Timothy was also timid and shy, an introvert. Many verses (such as 2 Timothy 1:7–8; 2:1; 3:14–15; 4:5) reveal that even after more than 15 years of training, Paul still had to tell him, "Get up! Don't be shy! Don't be timid! Don't be afraid."

Timothy was not, by makeup and temperament, a natural leader. If you had called him to lead, he would have said, "Please, not me. Let someone else do it. I will follow." He didn't want to be in the limelight. How different from so many today! People murmur and grumble and fight for position, saying, "I've been in the ministry for 10 years and I'm not yet promoted!" "I'm better able to teach than this fellow. Why has he been made a leader and I haven't?" "Look at her! She's teaching, but I have a better degree!" We live with all kinds of such imaginations about ourselves. May we learn from Timothy!

In his book *Spiritual Leadership*, J. Oswald Sanders quotes A. W. Tozer, perfectly stating why Timothy was a good candidate to take on the ministry after Paul:

> A true and safe leader is likely to be the one who has no desire to lead, but is forced into a position of leadership by the inward pressure of the Holy Spirit and the press of external situation.

Such were Moses and David and the Old Testament prophets. I think there was hardly a great leader from Paul to the present day but was drafted by the Holy Spirit for the task, and commissioned by the Lord of the Church to fill a position he had little heart for. I believe it might be accepted as a fairly reliable rule of thumb that the man who is ambitious to lead is disqualified as a leader. The true leader will have no desire to lord it over God's heritage, but will be humble, gentle, self-sacrificing and altogether as ready to follow as to lead, when the Spirit makes it clear that a wiser and more gifted man than himself has appeared.[2]

God had called Timothy, and he must now step out in faith and be bold in the work of the Lord.

It may sound as if the odds are stacked against Timothy, but please see how his age, weakness and even his personality did not qualify or disqualify him for being a servant of God. The one determining and sustaining factor was the fact that *he had been called by God for the work of the ministry.* It was this that qualified him before God and man, and the reason Paul entrusted the church at Ephesus to him during his first arrest. In Philippians 2:20–22, Paul wrote of him:

I have no one else like him, who takes a genuine interest in your welfare. For everyone looks out for his own interests, not those of Jesus Christ. But you know that Timothy has proved himself, because as a son with his father he has served with me in the work of the gospel.

Are you called? Take courage in the truth of that call, and let it be your assurance. Despite the weaknesses you see in yourself or the difficulty that may come in the work, you can fulfill the purposes of God. For "God, who has *called you* . . . is faithful" (1 Corinthians 1:9, emphasis mine).

What Is a Call?

We see that Timothy was called by God and because of this call was found adequate as a worker to carry on the ministry after Paul. But what exactly is a call?

When my wife, Gisela, gave her life to the Lord as a teenager in Germany, she felt this distinct burden come on her heart a short time later: *I am called by the Lord to be a missionary. I want nothing else for my life.*

As a symbol of her call, she took a South American coin inscribed with the head of a tribe (like our coins with Gandhi's or Nehru's image), punched a hole into it and tied it with a string. She wore the coin as a necklace, and every time she stood in front of the mirror to wash her face or comb her hair, the first thing she saw was not her own face but the coin hanging there on her neck. It served as a constant reminder to the call the Lord placed on her life. Because of that call, her life was different now. She could not be like other people.

When Gisela went for her higher studies and dozens of her friends were involved with many activities, even good ones, she said to herself, *They can, but I cannot.* Her character and decisions—even down to buying clothes—were directed by her call. When her sister bought new things with money given the girls by their parents, Gisela would not spend it on herself. Instead, she sent the money to a Wycliffe missionary who had been translating the Bible in South America for many years. Why? Because she knew there was a call upon her life—to live differently and serve her Lord.

What, then, is a call? It is a burden that never leaves you. Nothing can shake that burden from your heart or mind.

It affects every part of your life, and by it you see all else. It inspires you to joyfully forsake all to pursue it, just like the man who found the pearl of great price and sold everything he had just to buy it (see Matthew 13:45–46). It continually urges from within your heart, pleading like Paul to Timothy, "But for you, be different. Others can have freedom. What they are doing is not wrong. But for you, be different. There is a higher call that you must follow."

I, too, heard the call of the Lord on my life while I was attending a mission conference in Bangalore when I was 16 years old. That night—the night of all nights that I never will forget—Jesus impressed on my heart the burden to commit my life to serve Him.

I will never forget how I wept throughout the evening, my pillow soaked wet with my tears. With fear and trembling, I knelt beside my bed and prayed, "O Lord, I have nothing to give up. I don't have any degrees. I have no money. I am not tall and big and healthy. I have no name. I have nothing, not even a reputation. Nothing. All I have is this fragile, little body of mine. Do You want it? I give it to You."

That was the beginning of my journey. It was because of that call that numerous times I wept on the streets of Rajasthan as I watched the crowds of people, young and old, who did not know of my Jesus' love. I was so gripped with the reality of so many lost souls. No wonder when I had typhoid and my colleagues left me in the Ajmer government hospital—never telling me when they would come back, leaving me without relatives, friends or anyone—I never asked who would take care of me. No wonder I never asked where my salary was. I had nothing to ask for; I just had my call. The call gave me absolute assurance that no matter what problems, setbacks or suffering I faced, God would fulfill His plan in my life.

Fruit of Knowing You're Called

When we have received a call from the Lord, our lives will bear the fruit of it—the fruit of assurance, ownership, pure motivation and seeking only the Lord's approval.

Assurance. When you know God has called you, you walk in that assurance. No person or difficulty can deter you or make you turn back. You are certain that He who called you will be faithful.

Consider Joseph as one example. He stayed assured of the promise of God even when his brothers threw him into the pit and sold him to the Egyptians (see Genesis 37:23–28). He ended up in the dungeon and many years were lost, but nonetheless, nothing could stop his brothers from bowing down to him as prime minister of Egypt for 43 years! Why? Because the Lord had placed that call upon his life!

Ownership. Not only is there that absolute assurance in the life of one called by God, but there is a sense of personal ownership as well. A friend of mine illustrates this perfectly through the difference between a nurse and a mother.

A gifted and able nurse wakes each morning, gets ready for the day and goes to the hospital where she works. All day long she takes care of a sick baby. She periodically checks in on the child, feeds it and gives it medicine, making sure it has everything it needs. But when five o'clock comes, she leaves her job as a nurse and returns home. Taking care of that child is her profession, a salaried job.

The baby's mother, on the other hand, sits there night and day, not even leaving the baby's bedside to take a bath. She stands watch over her little baby *because that is her call.* She is the mother.

The difference between someone who is called and someone who does something because it is a profession is this sense of ownership over the work. The one who is called says, "It is my Jesus' kingdom. It is my burden. If I receive some kind of financial help, that's great. If I do not, no problem. I don't care. I will do it anyway." It is the call that gives you the motivation to journey on. Salary and benefits do not compel you; difficulties do not sway you. The knowledge that God is faithful and that He has called you is enough.

Pure motivation. Those who know they are called serve because of the knowledge of that calling, not because of the benefits they may be able to receive in the ministry or because of the salary they are provided. If your salary were stopped and your benefits discontinued or if nobody encouraged you through the provision of material things, would you continue the journey, saying, "I will keep on going as long as I can until, though I fall and die, I have finished my job"? I am honestly asking you: What would your response be?

When we are motivated by the knowledge of our calling, it also affects our personal lives and our relationships with those we serve with. Oftentimes, "the ministry" is marked by bickering, murmuring, jealousy, arrogance, comparison of self with others and internal strife. Hundreds of workers are destroyed along the way because they rationalize and justify that kind of behavior. The character of such a workman is fallen and flawed, seeking and motivated by something other than the calling of God. The person who knows he is called by the Lord acts differently.

The Lord's approval. The person who knows he has been called by the Lord for the work of the ministry seeks only the Lord's approval in all the work he does. In 2 Timothy 1:3 (TLB), Paul says, "My only purpose in life is to please him." Is that your goal too? Is pleasing God the compelling motivation of your life?

The Moravian movement of the 18th century, founded by Count N.L. von Zizendorf, has the following inscription on its seal: "Our Lamb has conquered. Let us follow Him." In the middle of the seal is a little lamb carrying a flag with a cross across it.

The Moravian movement was known for its commitment and zeal in preaching the Gospel. It was said that for every church at home in Germany, they had three more overseas. The church was a fishing pond from which they sent out missionaries.

Earlier in his life, Count Zizendorf had been strongly drawn to the classical pursuits of art, music, painting and the acquisition of riches. But one day he was so gripped with the reality of Christ dying on the cross for him that he gave his life completely to Him and heard His call to serve Him. It was out of that call that he wrote, "I have one passion. It is He, He alone."

Is Jesus your sole passion?

Do you know you have been called by Him for the work of the ministry? Does your life show the reality of that calling and burden? May we all seek to please Him alone, that all of our decisions, emotions and daily steps would be controlled by this one factor: "I am called by the Lord. He has chosen me. I am not my own, but His. I will follow Him all the days of my life."

Has He called you? Does your service reflect it? *Can He count on you?*

life of integrity

In the American form of government, the most powerful and influential group of people next to the president is the Senate. I once heard the story of one particular senator who was known for being an honest and God-fearing politician. Everywhere he went, people would ask him why he was so different from most politicians, why he would not compromise and why he gave such high priority to living by principle. To answer their questions, he told the following story.

One morning he and his father took their fishing poles and worms and started fishing on a lake. The guidelines that came with their license said that they could keep only the fish that were caught after noon (in the United States you must have a license to fish in the lakes).

For quite some time they patiently waited for a catch. Suddenly the boy felt a tug on his line. "Daddy, daddy," he cried out, "fish!"

His father helped him pull the line in, revealing a large, beautiful fish flopping on the end of the line.

"I caught a big fish!" cried the boy excitedly. "We can cook it, Daddy, and Mommy will be very happy."

But his father said, "Son, it is not yet noon."

"What do you mean?"

"The law says that we can only keep the fish we catch starting at exactly twelve noon. My son, it is not yet twelve o'clock."

"But, Daddy, nobody is here. We are the only people on this whole lake. Nobody will know!"

But his father stood strong. "Son, it is still five minutes before twelve. It is not yet noon."

"Oh, Daddy, please!" the boy cried. "It's only five minutes."

"My son, it may be only five minutes away, but I'm sorry, we cannot keep the fish."

The father took the fish and threw it back into the lake.

This example of his father's commitment to integrity, no matter how small or great the matter, impacted the boy so significantly that it is what he attributed his success as a politician to. He says that to this day, he still hears the voice of his father reminding him of the importance of integrity, that regardless of who sees or knows, he will consistently choose to do the right thing, no matter what the cost.

Integrity makes us or breaks us. Defined, the word *integrity* means "wholeness, the quality or state of being of sound moral principle, uprightness, honesty and sincerity."[1] Integrity is a consistency between private and public life, being what you claim to be and doing what you said you would do. You are on the inside what you are on the outside. Integrity refers to the consistency of character that matches words and actions, vision and choices, values and behaviors. It is life lived with consistency, and it is the reason why Paul was able to entrust the ministry into young Timothy's hands.

Timothy may have been young, sick, inexperienced, shy

and introverted, but there was something about him not found
in others. There may have been a thousand strong, educated,
aggressive and able leaders, but the torch was not passed into
any of their hands. Instead, it was given to skinny, timid
Timothy. Why? I am convinced it was because of this: Timothy
lived a life of integrity, committed to absolute honesty.

How do we know this? In 2 Timothy 1:3–5, Paul wrote to
Timothy, saying:

> I thank God, whom I serve, as my forefathers did, with a clear
> conscience, as night and day I constantly remember you in my
> prayers. . . . I have been reminded of your sincere faith, which
> first lived in your grandmother Lois and in your mother Eunice
> and, I am persuaded, now lives in you also.

Timothy's "sincere faith" and Paul's maintaining "a clear
conscience" stand out to me, revealing that both Paul and
Timothy had no secret agendas in the ministry. They served
from sincere hearts with honest motives. In 2 Corinthians 2:17,
Paul wrote, "Unlike so many, we do not peddle the word of
God for profit. On the contrary, in Christ we speak before God
with sincerity, like men sent from God" (emphasis mine). The
dictionary defines the word *sincere* as "being in reality what
it appears to be; having a character which corresponds with
the appearance; genuine; true; real."[2] It was this integrity that
made Paul's and Timothy's life and ministry effective.

Even the secular business world knows the value of the
man of integrity. A prominent businessman once said, "If I had
to name the one most important quality of a top manager, I
would say it is personal integrity, trustworthiness and sincerity
of promise. After that, uprightness in finances. Third, faithfulness in the discharge of duty. Fourth, loyalty in service. And

fifth, honesty in speech." How much greater is integrity valued in the kingdom of God! "The man of integrity walks securely, but he who takes crooked paths will be found out" (Proverbs 10:9). And Psalm 51:6 (NKJV) echoes the importance God places on this character trait: "Behold, You desire truth in the inward parts."

These verses show that God desires His children to wear no masks and live with no pretenses. When we live a life of complete integrity, we follow God's path and walk under His blessings. "The integrity of the upright guides them, but the unfaithful are destroyed by their duplicity [or pretense]" (Proverbs 11:3).

I want to highlight four areas of our lives and ministry that must be marked by absolute integrity.

Integrity in Your Finances

Handling money is often the primary area in which integrity is found lacking, and unfaithful stewardship is the number one destroyer of so many in ministry today.

In Matthew 6:24, Jesus said, "You cannot serve both God and Money." Notice He did not say, "You cannot serve both God and the devil," or "You cannot serve both God and the world." He specifically contrasted the impossibility of serving both God and money at the same time. (In fact, Jesus talked more about money than about heaven and hell!)

It really is not money that is the problem, but *the love of* money. Paul told Timothy that "the love of money is a root of all kinds of evil" (1 Timothy 6:10). Notice it does not say "some evil," but "*all* kinds of evil."

How does integrity in finances translate into everyday life? As an example, imagine that headquarters sends you out on a ministry trip at the last minute. Because of the short notice, there are no more second-class seats available on the train, and so you must travel first-class. When you get to the station and go to the counter to buy your ticket, however, you find that there is now one second-class ticket available because of a late cancellation. You gladly take the second-class seat and board the train for your journey.

You know that everyone at headquarters knew there was no other option but for you to travel by first-class and that it would cost 1,000 rupees. But now, through this unexpected turn of events, you had to spend only 400 rupees. You have 600 rupees left. Are you going to keep the balance or return the extra to the office?

Your answer is a measure of your financial integrity.

I write the following with remorse and shame. When I was around 18 years old, I would look at the stamp on the envelope of each letter I received to see if there was a cancellation seal on it. If there was no seal, I would wet the stamp with water, carefully pull it off and dry it flat in a book. Quietly I would say to myself, "Hallelujah, the Lord provided an extra stamp for me to use." I had it made, I thought, because the post office had not canceled the stamp! Later I would put glue on the stamp, stick it onto another envelope and mail the letter. That way I did not have to pay the two rupees for the cost of a stamp.

Then the Lord began to shed light on the issue. I felt His conviction that what I was doing was wrong. I did not argue because I realized I was a thief, taking from the post office what I had not paid for.

How did I respond to the conviction the Lord brought to my heart? I went to the post office and bought a bunch of stamps—many more than I had ever stolen by taking those uncanceled stamps from envelopes—and tore them all up and destroyed them. Why? To clear my conscience from the times I did not walk in integrity.

I want to ask you: Has there ever been a time in your ministry, perhaps through some transaction with a bank or a barber, that you have personally received even as little as one rupee? How about one kilo of tomatoes? One piece of clothing? One sari? One shirt? Has anyone ever given you anything as a commission or gift because you did business with him on behalf of the ministry or organization you represent? Did you take it? If you have, I can tell you what it means: You are not walking in integrity.

My brothers and sisters, you can fast all you want, pray all you want, praise the Lord all you want and pretend to be godly all you want, but unless you are conducting your ministry with absolute honesty and integrity in your finances, your family and ministry can never receive the spiritual blessings of God.

If you need to repent in this area, please do it now. Make this commitment: "Lord, from now on I want to be different. Teach me to walk in integrity in all things." Then make restitution and pay back the money you know was not yours to keep.

Integrity in Your Work

Often while traveling in Delhi, I will see a man selling lottery tickets at the major junctions. He rides around on a bicycle with his little bullhorn, and he is but skin and bones. What is interesting about this man is the time he begins his work in the morning. He knows that at 6:00 A.M. all the buses leave for their various destinations, so he makes sure he is up and ready to work by then, riding around and honking his horn early each morning. He knows that if he does not seize the time and opportunity, his chances for selling tickets and making a profit will significantly decrease. Even though his wife may run after him, saying, "You didn't drink your tea," he replies back, "I'll drink it later; now I must go." He knows the task at hand and is committed to making the most of his day and business opportunities.

When we think about how the living God has called us into His service and has set us responsible over the work of the eternal kingdom, how can we not be even more committed than this man? How can we not wake just as early, just as focused and intense, ready to set our hand to the plow, when we are in the urgent business of rescuing the perishing? Have we forgotten these things?

Let me ask you, when do you begin your work? Nine or ten o'clock? Does the sun have to come up and beat on you before you even think about getting up? Maybe once you are up, do you slowly take your time to have your tea and read the newspaper before you go to the post office and talk with friends for a while? Then, in the evening, maybe out of guilt, you take the one hour you have left to ride your bicycle somewhere and give out a couple of Gospel tracts before returning home to go to sleep. Does this describe you?

If you are a Bible college teacher, how many hours do you spend preparing and praying so that your teaching is not like old, stale bread but is fresh with anointing and new understanding? I cannot emphasize enough the seriousness of integrity in your work and the way you conduct things when no one is watching or questioning you. God sees when you remain faithful in these things and is pleased.

I am not saying you should start working every day at five in the morning and not stop until ten at night. The issue is that your life itself is an offering given continually to the Lord as *He* demands it. Serving God is not employment. It is not an eight-to-five job. It is a privilege. Therefore, "Whatever you do, do your work heartily, as for the Lord rather than for men, knowing that from the Lord you will receive the reward of the inheritance. It is the Lord Christ whom you serve" (Colossians 3:23–24, NASB).

Why did God choose David to be the king of Israel (see 1 Samuel 16:5, 10–11)? One reason is that when nobody was watching him—not his father, not his mother, not his brothers—he was faithful with his work. When he was out there in the wilderness watching over his father's sheep and a wild animal approached, he did not say, "What can I do? I'm just a small boy and my stronger brothers aren't here to rescue the sheep. I'll just climb a tree and watch, even if the animal destroys part of the flock." No, David went after the wild animals, killed them and saved his father's sheep. He was faithful with his task. Even though there was no one looking over his shoulder to see what he did every minute of the day, he understood the importance of walking in integrity before His Lord. We must live with the same understanding and let it direct the way we spend our day and do our work.

My brothers and sisters, we are not our own. We have been bought with a price (see 1 Corinthians 6:19–20). And not only were we bought with a high price, but we have been called to be the servants of God. Therefore, let us live accordingly, honoring God by the decisions we make in the work He has entrusted to us. Let us be faithful stewards of our time and work, making the most of each day and opportunity the Lord gives us.

Loyalty Is Crucial

In Psalm 78:8, God has some painful, emotional words about His people, concerning another area in which integrity is important—the loyalty in our hearts to that which God has called us. Unfortunately, God says of His children that their "hearts were not loyal to [Him]."

Paul also experienced the pain and betrayal of disloyalty when Demas, a dear colaborer in the work of God, deserted him and the ministry because "he loved this world" (2 Timothy 4:10).

God puts great emphasis on the loyal heart, advising the wise man to "let not *loyalty* and faithfulness forsake you; bind them about your neck, write them on the tablet of your heart. So you will find favor and good repute in the sight of God and man" (Proverbs 3:3–4, RSV, emphasis mine). Through this verse we see that loyalty is not just something that is cooked up, but weaved into the fiber of our hearts. And, by nature, loyalty is often costly. Woodrow Wilson, the 28th president of the United States, said it perfectly—"Loyalty means nothing unless it has at its heart the absolute principle of self-sacrifice."

Look at your life. Are you loyal to the church or organization that the Lord has called you to serve? Do you criticize the leaders behind their backs? Do you go around like Korah, spreading rumors and asking questions that cause confusion and doubt (see Numbers 16)? Are you someone who imagines and propagates evil things about the ministry?

Once in a while somebody comes to me to tell me bad things about our ministry. Willingly I listen, and when that person is finished I say, "Is there anything else? Is that all you can tell me about us? I can tell you about 10 hours' worth of problems we have here in our organization. If these are all the problems you know about, then we are doing quite well!"

Think about your own family. It is a small unit, yet how much misunderstanding, pain, anguish and trouble do you face each day? How many times has your mother cried or your father become angry? How many times have you been hurt or punished for things you never did, said or thought?

Now think about a large organization with people from numerous diverse backgrounds, speaking many different languages and eating snakes, dogs, oxtail, various colors of rice or chicken gizzard. You can imagine the many conflicts that arise from such incredibly complicated backgrounds coming to live together!

You might think life should be as it will be when we are raptured and sitting in heaven. Wake up! This is earth. We are still living here in the flesh with all its struggles, failures and misunderstandings. So when someone comes to you complaining about a Christian leader or his ministry, stop him and say, "What are you talking about? How do you know this? Did you talk to that leader? Have you ever spent one day fasting and praying for him and his family?" Often the first thing we do is complain, criticize and tear people down without taking even one day to stand in the gap, pray and agonize before the Lord for them. G.K. Chesterton summed it up well when he said, "We are all in the same boat in a stormy sea, and we owe each other a terrible loyalty."

Are you maintaining a clear conscience in the area of loyalty to the organization or church and people the Lord has called you to serve? Search your heart. If corrections must be made, I pray you will do that.

Integrity in Your Speech

"If anyone considers himself religious and yet does not keep a tight rein on his tongue, he deceives himself and his religion is worthless" (James 1:26). How powerful are our words!

Are you careful with the words you allow to come out of your mouth? So often, either by intent or carelessness, we do such great harm by the words we speak. We have forgotten that "the tongue has the power of life and death" (Proverbs 18:21), making it so important for the servant of God to hold to integrity in the things he says and the words he listens to.

When you report things that you have heard, even things that are true, what is your motive for sharing? Why do you say what you say? Is it because the Lord has given you the conviction to build up, strengthen and help others? Or are you trying to put someone down, condemn another or climb the ladder through someone else's fall?

Some of the deepest regrets of my life are decisions I made, opinions I formed, people I rejected and doors I closed because I believed and listened to gossip from those who were telling things with the wrong motive.

Over the past two or three years, I have made a covenant with myself not to arrive at any decision unless I have firsthand information that has been carefully investigated. Even then I will not jump quickly to make decisions. Why? Because in the past so many people have been hurt, so many friends lost and so many opportunities wasted simply because I listened to people without thinking deeply about what I was being told.

The movement you are a part of—your Bible college, your coworkers' lives, your children's future and everything you touch—will likewise be destroyed if you are not careful with what you hear and what you say. This destruction will not happen for lack of education, skill or infrastructure, but for lack of love. Just a little bit of evil talk, just a little gossip, maligning others and cooking up negative stories can do an immense amount of harm, not only to others but to yourself as well.

Please realize that when you participate in gossip, you open the door to the devil's devices. It is a wide-open door, welcoming demons to come in like a flood. Even when someone has failed, you must keep yourself from evil talk. It is not your business to tell others about it or even listen to it; instead, talk to God about it and fast and pray for the individual. Make a covenant with your ears and mouth never to tell others negative things or to listen to negative things. May we never dishonor the call the Lord has given us by participating in any kind of talk that does not honor Him!

Marked by Integrity

Many start the race, but only those who abide by the rules laid out beforehand will receive the prize. Integrity is the rule of ministry. We must be an honest people, full of integrity in our financial responsibilities, our work, our loyalty to others and our speech. By living this, we can be sure to stay on the narrow road, and all that we do will not only be blessed by God, but bring glory to Him as well. Live by 2 Corinthians 8:21: "For we are taking pains to do what is right, not only in the eyes of the Lord but also in the eyes of men."

Be known by all men for your life of integrity.

four

by His Spirit

"Then Saul, still breathing threats and murder against the disciples of the Lord, went to the high priest and asked letters from him to the synagogues of Damascus, so that if he found any who were of the Way, whether men or women, he might bring them bound to Jerusalem. As he journeyed he came near Damascus, and suddenly a light shone around him from heaven. Then he fell to the ground, and heard a voice saying to him, 'Saul, Saul, why are you persecuting Me?' " (Acts 9:1–4, NKJV).

What a terrifying and incredible experience! Saul, the great teacher of the law who could sharply dissect and silence anyone who came against him, lies flat on the ground, thrown off of his horse by some mysterious, bright light. Those around him, trembling and astonished, saw nothing, only heard a mighty voice from heaven. Saul walks away alive, but blind. The great Saul is now humbly led around by hand, not quite sure what just happened to him or why (see Acts 9:5–9).

The purpose of this experience was explained to him shortly afterward: "Brother Saul, the Lord Jesus, who appeared to you on the road as you came, has sent me that you may receive your sight and *be filled with the Holy Spirit"* (Acts 9:17, NKJV, emphasis mine). From his first experience with the living God, Paul knew of the incredible power of the Holy Spirit, for it was by His work that his heart was softened and changed from one of stone to one of flesh. It was by the same power that this man, who once hunted down Christians to kill them by brutal murders, became the key individual to seeing the kingdom of God spread across the whole known world in the first century.

In every shipwreck, every arguing crowd, every time he stood before the Jewish leaders and every letter he wrote to the churches, Paul knew the power of the Holy Spirit in his life and ministry in a very real and great way. He understood the dire importance of being filled with the Spirit, which is why within the first sentences of his last letter to Timothy, he reminds him to "fan into flame the gift of God, which is in you through the laying on of my hands. For God did not give us a spirit of timidity, but a spirit of power" (2 Timothy 1:6–7).

Imagine being Timothy. For years, you have been instructed by Paul, receiving his correction and encouragement and seeing the growth in your own life as well as in the ministry. You sit there reading Paul's letter, knowing that the days have grown harder and once again he has written from prison. As you read, you sense an urgency in his words and realize what he is doing—he is passing the torch . . . to you! Paul's race is over—now you must run, and run hard.

Can you imagine the pressure on Timothy? How this already shy and introverted boy must have felt as he held that letter in his hands, pondering the journey that lay before him!

Paul understood. He knew that what lay before Timothy was a task humanly impossible, as is all Christian service. That is why he directs Timothy's eyes not onto himself, but on the priceless gift of God within him—the Holy Spirit, who alone is able to work through Timothy, do the ministry and carry out the responsibilities that are now entrusted to him.

Listen to the hope and energy in Paul's words as he passes the torch onto Timothy, saying, "My dear son! God has called you. I know your faith is sincere. I know that your heart is pure. Now remember the gift of God within you! He has put His Spirit inside you, and it is not one of fear or timidity, but of power! Now fan that into flame and run, Timothy, run!"

Paul's words were not a suggestion; this was not just one of his "tips in serving God well." It was of *absolute necessity* that Timothy fan into flame the gift within him and minister by the power of the Holy Spirit. All of us called as servants of God must—absolutely must—heed the instruction of Paul. We *must* be filled with power from on high.

Being "Full of the Spirit"

Unfortunately, the power of the Holy Spirit is one of those subjects that people in many parachurch or nondenominational organizations tend to avoid, often because of the extremism found in some sections of Christianity and their teaching on the Holy Spirit. Emotional upheaval and radical manifestations have caused many evangelicals to shy away from the balanced teaching of Scripture on this crucial subject.

We must never forget that even the Lord Jesus Christ—God in flesh and the perfect, sinless Savior—had to be anointed with the Holy Spirit before starting His ministry on earth (see Matthew 3:16–17; Acts 10:38). His powerful ministry was not just something granted to Him by virtue of the fact that He was the Son of God. It was by the power of the Holy Spirit that He healed the sick, gave sight to the blind, made the lame walk, raised the dead and preached the kingdom's arrival.

And it was for this reason that Jesus "commanded [His disciples] . . . to wait for the Promise of the Father, 'which,' He said, 'you have heard from Me; for John truly baptized with water, but you shall be baptized with the Holy Spirit not many days from now. . . . You shall receive power when the Holy Spirit has come upon you; and you shall be witnesses to Me in Jerusalem, and in all Judea and Samaria, and to the end of the earth' " (Acts 1:4–5, 8, NKJV).

Not too long before leaving them with this instruction, Jesus came to these disciples and passed a torch on to them, saying, "Go and make disciples of all nations, baptizing them in the name of the Father and of the Son and of the Holy Spirit, and teaching them to obey everything I have commanded you" (Matthew 28:19–20). But when Jesus came to them, they were much in the state that Timothy was probably in when reading Paul's letter.

For three years they walked with Jesus, sharing in the joy and thrill of His ministry. They stood beside Him as He touched the blind man's eyes and rejoiced in amazement as sight came to him. But now things were different. Jesus had been crucified, they had fled in fear, Peter had denied the Lord and they had lost all hope to the point that they were returning to their fishing boats (see Luke 24:21; John 21:3–4). And now Jesus is telling *them* to go into *all* the world and do *all* the things He had done while with them? How impossible this task was! It must have sounded absurd. The disciples probably responded, "Jesus, we understand what You are saying, but physically You have been with us all these years. Now You say You are going back to the Father. How are we going to do this work without You?"

The answer? It wasn't going to be without Him.

He was sending the Holy Spirit, the One who would now lead them and give them the power to carry on the ministry. "Surely I am with you always, to the very end of the age" (Matthew 28:20).

Indeed, the Lord knew they would never be able to do what He asked in their own power. He had told them earlier that that was absolutely impossible (see John 15:4). That is why He commanded them to wait until they were baptized with the Holy Spirit and had received His power for ministry.

The same is true for us today. The power of the Holy Spirit is absolutely necessary. Why? Because the work to be done is not in the realm of flesh and blood alone. Our task is super-natural. And it is only by the Spirit's power that we can accom-plish the task our Lord and Savior left for us. It was the only way that Peter, the one who was so afraid of men that he ran away denying Christ, stood up with courage in the face of mar-tyrdom to declare the Gospel and led thousands to repentance (see Acts 2). The power of the Holy Spirit is what enabled Stephen, a simple layperson in the Church, to single-handedly speak on behalf of the kingdom and then lay down his life for the faith (see Acts 7). And it is what enables and equips us for the task today, no matter how great or how small.

Consider how the apostles chose the men who would serve food to the widows? Such a seemingly simple job, yet the neces-sary qualification was that the men were *full of the Spirit and wisdom*" (Acts 6:3, emphasis mine).

Why did these servants need to be filled with the Spirit? Because their service would never be authentic without the Holy Spirit's power. I am afraid that much of the work done today in the name of serving God is nothing but a work of the flesh, a struggle to perform supernatural work by mere human effort. Someday the fire of God's testing will burn to ashes all work done by human strength alone. Ministry must not be "by might nor by power, but by [His] Spirit" (Zechariah 4:6, NKJV). This is the only kind of work that will survive into eternity.

If men who waited on tables needed to be filled with the Holy Spirit, how much more do those who stand before multitudes bound by powers of darkness and destined for hell need to be!

The book of Acts tells us the story of how these once weak and scurrying disciples went out in the power of the Holy Spirit and fulfilled the task the Lord Jesus left them with. Story after story, we see how they were filled with the Holy Spirit and went out in power to proclaim the Good News to their world. No wonder these people had a reputation as world revolutionaries (see Acts 17:6)! Can you imagine if these disciples had faced the intense opposition we read about in the book of Acts *without* the power and supernatural guidance of the Holy Spirit? You can understand why Jesus told them to wait for the power of the Holy Spirit before doing any ministry.

Let me ask you—are you one who waits? Before going out for any ministry, are you taking the time to wait before the Lord and be filled with power from on high?

My brothers and sisters, today in the Indian subcontinent we are faced with the same circumstances the early Church faced—and maybe even worse. Not a week goes by when dozens of missionaries, pastors and evangelists are not beaten, abused and taken to prison. In recent years, we have heard of hundreds of churches being burned and missionaries brutally murdered. The opposition is increasing as never before. How on earth are we to face this hostile environment and be able to fulfill the call of the Lord to see millions turn to Him?

The answer, once again, is only by the power of the Holy Spirit!

We need men and women "full of the Spirit and wisdom" (see Acts 6:3), brothers and sisters who are bold and courageous to face demons and hell, who will do the exploits of God otherwise impossible if it were not for this power made available to us!

We need men and women recognized by heaven and who cause hell to tremble by the authority and the power they walk in because of the Holy Spirit (see Acts 19:13–16)!

We need men and women filled with the Holy Spirit and walking with spiritual discernment, by faith and not by sight, just as Paul did in Acts 16, when, by the counsel of the Holy Spirit, he traveled to Europe instead of Asia! One of the saddest crises we face in the Body of Christ today is a lack in this very area.

We desperately need men and women who not only understand doctrine, theory and teaching on the Holy Spirit, but who experience the reality of the Holy Spirit and His fullness in their daily lives and ministries, who know the precious gift of God within them that is able to set the captives free and who do just that!

Are you this kind of person? Are your life and ministry daily empowered by the gift of God within you, the same Spirit who raised Christ Jesus from the dead? My brothers and sisters, please, if not, cry out to God for this power so that you might rescue the perishing and win this generation for Christ. Stir up the gift of God within you!

Power for Ministry

There are literally hundreds of stories of our workers on the field facing tremendous opposition. Through the power of the Holy Spirit, they have been able to face incredible hostility and do the work of God, just as we read about in the book of Acts. The story of one brother is a perfect example of the need to be filled with the Spirit and the power provided for us when we are.

As one brother was preaching the Gospel before a large crowd, an opposition group of men climbed onto the stage, bringing him a man actually bound in chains. The man was acting out of control, as you would expect from a demon-possessed person. The leader of the group took the micro-phone from the brother and said in a taunting tone of voice, "You preach about Jesus who healed the sick and performed miracles. Now we've brought you a madman bound in chains. You claim your Jesus can set people free and heal them. So show us!"

The group had brought the man in order to create confusion and destroy the work that God was doing in that place. And, to be sure, the crowd was sent into an uproar.

Meanwhile, the Holy Spirit gave discernment to this dear brother, telling him that this chain-bound man was not actually sick or demon-possessed at all. These men had created a trap to make a mockery of the evening and to show contempt for the name of Jesus.

Through the Holy Spirit, the Lord instructed the preacher to stretch out his hand toward the chained man, which he did. At that moment the man—who in actuality was totally well and only acting demon-possessed to cause trouble—lost control and became enraged. He snapped the chains that were wrapped around him and began to move away from the group.

The fanatics who had come to disturb the meeting realized something had happened that they now could not control. One of them dropped to his knees at the feet of the preacher and cried out, "We came to hurt you, to make a mockery of the name Jesus and to beat you up, but now we know that your God is greater. Please help this man!"

The brother took the microphone to calm the crowd and explain the situation. Then he told the fanatics to bring the now demon-possessed man to him. With difficulty, they captured him and brought him to the preacher. With that large crowd as a witness, he explained the Gospel. Then, in the name of the Lord Jesus Christ, he laid his hand on the man and commanded the powers of darkness to leave him. Instantly, the Lord set the man free.

You can imagine the impact that the freeing of this man had on the crowd! Hundreds gave their lives to Christ that night, including some of the men who had come to mock our brother and disturb the meeting.

This brother was given discernment from the Holy Spirit, was instructed by the Holy Spirit, was made courageous to face the demonic forces by the Holy Spirit and set this captive free—all by the power of the Holy Spirit. Can you imagine how the situation would have turned out if not for the precious gift of God within this man?

This kind of story is nothing new or strange. Just as events like this happened in the book of Acts, so it happens today. "Jesus Christ is the same yesterday and today and forever" (Hebrews 13:8). The Holy Spirit who worked in mighty ways through the early Christians does the same thing today, if only we will believe and yield to His power in our ministry.

The Evidence of Being Filled

As stated earlier, there is a lot of confusion today over the baptism of the Holy Spirit and the evidence of it. But I caution you:

> The wrapping should never be mistaken for the gift. The Holy Spirit Himself is the Gift of the Risen Lord to His Church. When He falls upon people, it may be with shouts of Hallelujah, tears of joy and the gift of tongues, or it may be quietly, silently and without much emotion. Temperaments vary, and the Spirit of God (unlike many Christians) is willing to adapt Himself to each temperament. It is foolish therefore to expect that others should receive the Gift in the same wrapping in which we

received Him—whether spectacular or commonplace. Only babies are taken up with the tissue-paper in which a gift comes to them. Mature men recognize that the gift itself is more important than the wrapping. The Apostle Paul was converted through a vision of Jesus. But he did not preach that all needed a similar vision. . . . He recognized that it was the inner reality that mattered, in whatever wrapping it might come. So too with the fullness of the Holy Spirit.[1]

This is especially true these days when so much false teaching is being promoted from some of the Western nations. We need to be extremely cautious and scriptural as we deal with this subject. The Holy Spirit always operates in line with the Word of God, for He Himself is the Author of it. We must search the Scriptures with the determination to follow the truth and not allow extremists or counterfeits to cause us to deny or delay the incredible promise of the power of the Holy Spirit that is made available for every child of God today.

In the early years of my ministry, I spoke according to my own ability and cleverness. Though people were impressed, inside I was drying up. I struggled without any overcoming life in me. I carried a lot of information in my head, but I was like a chandelier with the switch turned off. It looks nice, the bulbs are brand-new, the electrical cord intact, but the power needed to light it is missing.

One evening, before I was to speak in a meeting in Jammu Kashmir, I sat alone in my room and cried out in desperation to God. "Lord, I know my outline and I know my stories, but my heart is empty. I have no power. You promised to give me power. Please fill me with Your Holy Spirit and give me power to minister tonight."

I praise God for hearing my prayers that evening and filling me with the power of the Holy Spirit. The Lord did a mighty work that night. I don't even remember the message I spoke, but afterward hundreds of people came forward, weeping and crying out to God in repentance. Did I do it? No. Who did it? The Holy Spirit did it!

At Pentecost, the great work of seeing the world follow the Lord Jesus Christ began with flaming tongues and a rushing, mighty wind (see Acts 2:2–4). These were mere symbols of the presence of the Holy Spirit. In your life, as you are filled with the Holy Spirit, you will know without any shadow of doubt (whether quiet or loud) that you are empowered by the Holy Spirit.

What will be the evidence of this? Many people argue over it, but as George Verwer said, "I don't care how you get it, you'd just better get it!" Whether the evidence is speaking in tongues, jumping up and down or doing absolutely nothing, I cannot tell you. But I can tell you one thing: The empowering of the Holy Spirit will bring tremendous power for service in your life. You cannot effectively minister without it.

Equipped for the Challenge Today

Perhaps you can recall a time when you were filled with the power of the Holy Spirit. If you say, "I had that wonderful experience 20 years ago," I ask you, what about today? Do you have the experience of being filled with the Holy Spirit today? The past is past. The Bible exhorts us to be *continually* filled with the Holy Spirit (see Acts 13:52; Ephesians 5:18). Yesterday's experience is not enough; it is the daily walking in the Spirit that makes the difference.

This is why Paul urges Timothy to "fan into flame the gift of God" that he received when Paul laid his hands upon him. Paul is telling him not to rely on that one time but to be continually filled. It must be a daily, ongoing experience in his life and ministry.

My brothers and sisters, may we understand the seriousness of the call Christ has given to each of us. Let us not rely on our own ability or be kept at bay and hindered by our lack of ability or experience in the ministry. The Spirit of God within us is enough to "preach good tidings to the poor . . . heal the brokenhearted, to proclaim liberty to the captives, and the opening of the prison to those who are bound" (Isaiah 61:1, NKJV).

God has called you to this task. Now receive the instruction Christ gave to His disciples and that Paul gave to Timothy, and fan into flame the gift of God within you that you might go forth and accomplish the mission. May the power of the Holy Spirit be our portion as we enter into a new era of awesome challenge and opportunity in the work of God on the Indian subcontinent.

Oh, for the authentic baptism of the Holy Spirit!

living by
self-discipline

Vital to the servant of God's life and ministry is self-discipline. Without it, no army can win a war, no athlete can win the prize and no servant of God can move into the things God has for him. As J. Oswald Sanders said, "Only the disciplined person will rise to his highest power. He is able to lead because he has conquered himself."[1] No matter how able, educated or gifted a person is, he will never fulfill the call of God on his life without self-discipline.

It is interesting that Paul addresses this issue of self-discipline early on in his last words to Timothy, reminding him that God has given us "a spirit of . . . self-discipline" (2 Timothy 1:7).

This wasn't the first time Paul spoke of self-discipline. In his first letter to Timothy, he encouraged him to "discipline yourself for the purpose of godliness" (1 Timothy 4:7, NASB), and Paul set the example for him in this. In his letter to the church at Corinth, Paul said, "I *discipline* my body and make it my slave, so that, after I have preached to others, I myself will not be disqualified" (1 Corinthians 9:27, NASB, emphasis mine). He knew that in order to be effective in ministry and fulfilling the call of God, one must bring the outer man under control. And now, with Timothy taking Paul's place, he must step up in his own life of self-discipline.

In fact, all those who desire to follow Christ must come this way as well. If we are to be *disciples* of Christ, we must be people of self-*discipline*. Notice how *disciple* and *discipline* come from the same root word, showing us what type of people the Lord's servants must be.

Paul goes on further to liken the self-discipline of a servant of God with that of an athlete (see 2 Timothy 2:5), a farmer (see 2 Timothy 2:6) and a soldier (see 2 Timothy 2:4).

Consider how an athlete trains for the Olympics. The decision to compete is never made at the last minute—it always comes from a life lived year after year training in his particular event. From a young age, he awakes at an incredibly early hour, day after day, so that he can practice before school starts. After school he continues his training. Events and entertainment that others enjoy are sacrificed in light of the goal to one day compete in the Olympics. This discipline is engrained into the fabric of his life, and the sacrifices it demands are worth the goal he strives for.

Consider the life of a soldier. For weeks, he goes through intense training to prepare his body for some of the most severe physical challenges. He must be prepared to endure all circumstances and conditions. And so, day after day, drill after drill, he brings his body into submission so that he will be ready for whatever may come. His body aches, his muscles are sore and tired and his heart misses home, but nonetheless, he disciplines himself so that he can fulfill the purpose for which he was enlisted.

Consider the farmer. Day after day in the sun, he labors in the field, plowing up the dirt, removing the rocks and preparing the soil for seed. His time is given to carefully watching the crop so that bugs or birds don't come in and destroy it. Then harvesttime comes and from sunup to sundown, he labors to reap it all in before it is too late and spoils. No vacation is taken and there is no time for leisure or play. He has disciplined himself in order to get the maximum out of his crops.

This same kind of self-discipline must be evident in Timothy's life if he is to fulfill the purpose for which God has called him. All of the instruction Paul goes on to give Timothy further in this letter hinges greatly on this one factor. You see, self-discipline is like a mighty wind. If we set the sail of our life according to this wind rather than against it, we are able to go places and accomplish things that otherwise we would not. By it we either move onward or remain where we are.

There are many people who want to do great things for God. They may even be skilled and very able, but they never make it. Why? Because they reject self-discipline. It is self-discipline—not a person's wishes or dreams—that empowers him to accomplish great things.

And so it is with us. The road marked out before us is steep and narrow. It is a road of suffering, yet one that leads to "joy unspeakable and full of glory" (1 Peter 1:8, KJV). All along the way, there will be voices calling out from each side of us to forsake the narrow road and walk an easier path, one of less resistance and less self-discipline. This is where we must hear again the words of Paul—*but for you*, be different. Everything is permissible, but not all things are beneficial (see 1 Corinthians 6:12). What that brother or sister is doing or how they are living may be okay, *but for you*, there is a higher calling. Choose to be different. Remember the goal before you and discipline yourself so as to run in a way to reach the goal.

Self-discipline is like this: While others waste their time, you study and read. While others sleep, you get up and pray.

While others feast and enjoy, you take days to fast. While others take it easy, you work hard. While others lose their tempers or speak casually, you guard your temperament, your heart and your mouth, disciplining yourself to be sober and not to respond with anger, hatred or loose words. As Henry Wadsworth Longfellow, the 19th-century English poet, once said, "The heights by great men reached and kept were not attained by sudden flight. But they, while their companions slept, were toiling upward in the night."

But self-discipline is not just something we cook up from ourselves. In Galatians 5:22, we are told that self-control is one of the fruits of the Spirit. As you read through the rest of this chapter, I ask that you would please allow the Holy Spirit to search your heart for areas of your life that need self-discipline. Then ask Him to bear that fruit within your life, giving you the grace and power to submit to His ways and please the Lord.

Some Areas of Concern

Just as Timothy's success in the ministry hinged upon whether or not he implemented self-discipline in the different aspects of his life, so it is with us. What we have done in the past for God means little for tomorrow. We cannot ride off of the past. We cannot live in neutral and expect to coast into fulfilling the call of God on our lives. We must put ourselves in gear, allow the Holy Spirit to identify the areas of our lives that need self-discipline and then daily make the choice to take up our cross and follow Him.

Remember that the nature of discipline is doing the things we don't exactly *feel* like doing. If we always felt like doing certain things, no self-discipline would be needed. But please, do not view self-discipline as something we just must endure. Realize that it is a highway, taking us off the roads full of traffic and frequent stops and setting us on a clear, focused, straight path that enables us to do the most with our lives.

Through the years that I've lived and served in the ministry, I have learned the great importance of self-discipline in certain areas of life, which I highlight below. I pray that as you read through these things, your heart will be open to the correction and instruction of the Holy Spirit.

Time management. I mention this one first, because if how we spend our time is carefully managed, we will find that we can accomplish more than we ever realized.

Let me ask you, what are the hours of your day filled with? Are you careful to manage your time well? Do you get up on time and meet deadlines given to you? Are you setting aside times to fast and pray regularly? Do you use your time wisely? Do you know what you are going to do tomorrow? Next month? Next year?

If you are not able to discipline your time well, here is a simple practice that might help you. Buy a notebook and write the date at the top of each page for each day of the month. Down the side of each page, write the time and what you plan to do that day for each hour in the day. For example, "5:00 A.M.—wake up." From 5:00 A.M. to 7:00 A.M., schedule time for reading, studying and praying. This is the best time of the day to spend before God because it is often the quietest and when you can be alone without any disturbances.

Your life may be spiritually dry because you are not committed to disciplining your time. You may even find you are able to tell a half-truth and that your conscience is no longer sharp. You may be worse off right now than before you were born again. Why? You don't have a devotional life. You don't read your Bible faithfully and systematically every day. You don't take time to pray and seek the Lord. Outside you are smiling, but on the inside your heart is gone. You have not been disciplined in your time with God.

Why should you be disciplined with your time? Because you have a higher call. You are not a civilian. You are not free. You are under God's command, and your life has been given to Him.

Fasting and prayer. Systematic prayer, fasting and Bible study are prime essentials for having a fruitful life. Do you keep a list of names of people for whom you are praying? Are you praying for someone every day? Every week? Every month? If you feel you don't have time to pray, make the time. Evaluate the unnecessary things in your day, eliminate them and give utmost priority to fasting and prayer.

Studying and learning. What books are you reading right now? Are you disciplined to read at least one book every month? How many times have you read through the whole Bible? You may say, "I am too busy," but you must make time for these things. That which is most important to you will show by how your time is spent.

Finances. Do you keep a good record of the expenses in your life, disciplining yourself not to buy anything with money you don't have or buy things that you do not really need? Never borrow to buy a television, refrigerator, two-wheeler or car. Never borrow from anyone except in an emergency involving food or medicine. Be ruthlessly disciplined about avoiding debt.

Avoid unnecessary luxuries and don't be wasteful in spending money. There are dangers in times of ease and prosperity that can be avoided only by our deliberate act and commitment to stay disciplined in this area.

Maintaining relationships. Do you make the time to keep in touch with those individuals the Lord has placed in your life? I encourage you to stay connected with those you have met along your journey and be a source of encouragement for them. Don't be so focused on work that you forget people. Look out for others and take interest in the lives of those with whom you serve, remembering that you are part of the *family* of God. We all need each other.

Work ethic. Do you maintain the life of discipline in the workplace, making certain that you keep yourself from unnecessary and idle distractions and use your time at work to the maximum potential? Do you remember whom you work for—the King of kings, who has called you to a great task? Therefore, let us work diligently and as unto the Lord (see Colossians 3:17). I encourage you to keep a daily log of how your workday progresses and ask the Holy Spirit to help you keep focused and work diligently.

Temperament. Are you easily angered? Do you quickly get impatient with others? Our attitudes are so powerful and can either be used for good or for destruction. You must keep a handle on your temper. Don't just say, "This is the way God made me." An undisciplined temperament can only hurt you and others.

Developing gifts. Are you lazy, and because of that are not developing the gifts God has given you? Remember the parable of the talents—those with whom the Lord was pleased were those who multiplied the gifts He had given them, rather than burying them. Please, consider what gifts the Lord has given you and work to develop them and use them for His glory.

Stewardship. Are you disciplined in taking care of your possessions? God has entrusted certain things to your care. Do you consider God's property as your own and take good care of those things He has given? Don't take for granted what you have; take care of it. God trusts those who are faithful in little things.

Conversations. Do you keep a careful watch on your tongue and the things that you say? How about the things you allow your ears to hear? Do you believe the truth that "men will have to give account on the day of judgment for every careless word they have spoken" (Matthew 12:36)? The servant of God should not quarrel but must be a gentle servant to others. Let your words be full of grace, kindness and mercy.

Friendships. What kind of people are you making friends with? "Do not be misled: 'Bad company corrupts good character' " (1 Corinthians 15:33). What kind of friend are you? Are you one who is able to be trusted? Be the kind of friend you would like to have. Think of ways to affirm your love and commitment to others, even those who have made mistakes.

Look carefully at your character, attitudes and relationships to see if any areas need change, and then be disciplined to change them with the Lord's power. Although others take the easy road, you must choose the hard road. Consider this prayer and let it be your own:

> God, harden me against myself,
> the coward with pathetic voice
> who craves for ease and rest and joy.
> Myself, arch-traitor to myself,
> my hallowest friend,
> my deadliest foe,
> my clog, whatever road I go.[2]

I encourage you to be militantly disciplined and not to have pity on yourself. Those with the greatest impact on our world are those who lived disciplined lives. Vigorous discipline is the expression of the inner life and commitment to God. I encourage you to choose this road.

Where to Start

How do you become a disciplined person? It begins with a conviction from Romans 15:3 that "even Christ did not please himself." In the same way, we should not seek to please ourselves. This is the foundation. And here are a few suggestions of where to start in living a more disciplined life.

Begin with little things. Don't try to run or fly; start by walking, and even crawling if need be. Do the little things. A disciplined person will always seek to avoid making unnecessary work for others, so hang up your clothes, put your trash away and help with the children; don't wait for your wife or somebody else to do it.

Break the habit of procrastinating. Don't avoid challenging responsibilities, but welcome them and tackle them quickly. Don't say, "Tomorrow I'll do it. Later I'll find the time." Do them right away so that they are done. It is hard, but if you do this, you will find that things will be much easier in the end.

Be punctual for your appointments. It is a myth that important people should be late to meetings. If everyone has to wait for you, you are being undisciplined. Plan enough time into your schedule to ensure that you make all of your meetings on time.

Master your moods. Discipline yourself to deal with the feel-sad and feel-good moods throughout your day. Do not allow your feelings to influence your work negatively. Make your moods obey you.

Control your curiosity. It is difficult to do this in the Indian culture, but we should not busy ourselves trying to find out everybody's problems. If someone is talking to someone else on the phone and you can hear even just one word, move away to give him privacy. Don't try to listen. If a letter is lying on the table, don't read it or even try to figure out whose handwriting it is. You be concerned about your own business. Curiosity about other people's business can make you imagine things, and the devil will use that against you.

To grab something before God's timing is to spoil it. Therefore, we must learn to wait. Let us be a people known for our patience.

Many of these things cannot be changed overnight. Nothing changes instantly. We have developed patterns and habits from our culture and our own behavior, so be patient with yourself and others. Don't become angry with people who are struggling in these areas. Instead, go forward learning, growing and helping others. If you do so, you will be blessed along the way.

Our Guarding

Proverbs 25:28 gives us a serious warning—"Like a city whose walls are broken down is a man who lacks self-control." Just as Timothy had to be careful to live a disciplined life, so must you and I. If not, we open our lives and ministry to the plunder of the enemy. But by walking in the spirit of self-discipline the Lord has given us, we surround our lives with walls of protection that keep us and the ministry safe and well on our way to reach the finish line.

Don't be fooled and exposed to the enemy's tactics. *Live a disciplined life.*

courageous in battle

Speaking at the Harvard University commencement service on June 8, 1978, Aleksandr Solzhenitsyn asked this question: "Must one point out that from ancient times a decline in courage has been considered the first symptom of the end?"[1]

His statement is true. Courage is essential to every work, and without it no one can fulfill the call of the Lord upon his life. This is the reason why Paul urges Timothy in 2 Timothy 1:8, "Do not be ashamed to testify about our Lord, or ashamed of me his prisoner. But join with me in suffering for the gospel, by the power of God."

As Paul lay in prison and saw the future of the Church, he thought to himself, *I need someone who can run the race. The opposition will be unparalleled. There will be tremendous opposition. Many will be killed for their faith, while large numbers may deny the faith. Even now, this is happening.*

The question is: *Who will have the courage to stand and fight the battle, to rally those who are faithful and to march on?*

Timothy must be courageous. But how could he be the one to stand up strong and bold, rally the faithful and lead to victory in intense persecution?

Paul knew Timothy well. He knew he was by nature timid and shy. He knew that by human nature, we are sensitive to the opinions of others and how people see us. We all like to be well thought of. We like to be esteemed. I'm sure Timothy was no different.

But Timothy *must* be different.

If he was to take Paul's place, he must not be influenced by the sway of public opinion and caught up in what people thought about him. He could not be ashamed to testify about the Lord, despite what people thought. He must not shrink away from standing for the truth. He must not lack the courage by which every battle worth fighting moves forward. He who was once weak and shy could be so no longer. There had to be a deep conviction in him that would be the force to pull him away from the common man's battle and propel him forward in courage. But again, in himself Timothy was not much. How could he become the courageous one to lead the work undaunted and unashamed?

Timothy could only do so by remembering who he was— one called by God. The assurance of that conviction would give him the courage to endure. It was because of his call that he could be courageous and bold as a lion. Timothy plus the whole world would have been the minority, but Timothy plus God was the majority. He may have looked around and seen giants in the land that made him feel like a grasshopper, but he had to remember that *God had called him.*

David was one who remembered that God had called him. When he came against Goliath, he confidently declared, "You come against me with sword and spear and javelin, but I come against you in the name of the Lord Almighty, the God of the armies of Israel, whom you have defied. This day the Lord will hand you over to me, and I'll strike you down and cut off your head" (1 Samuel 17:45–46). This was not mere human boasting. God had called him, and in that calling he took courage.

A second reason Timothy could be courageous and bold was because *he had no hidden agenda.* His faith was sincere. He had only to bow his head before God and submit to His will. Inside, the young man bore the absolute conviction that even if all hell broke loose, he need not fear because he knew in his conscience that his heart was clean before God.

I will never forget a situation we found ourselves in some years ago. I received a call from the office in India saying that our nation's Home Ministry was sending a delegation from Delhi to investigate Gospel for Asia. The man leading the delegation was known to be the most difficult person in looking at every detail of an organization's books to find any corruption.

"Don't ask anyone for help to get out of this," I responded to the office staff. "Let this man do whatever he wants to do." Our confident statement was, "We have no skeletons in any closet. We have never done anything in secret, nor do we have any hidden agenda. Never have we done one thing wrong that I know of with this organization's finances. We are not afraid of anyone."

Like Timothy, we could be courageous because our hearts were honest before God. This was not vain, human boasting; rather, we had nothing to fear because we knew God was with us. And, indeed, the investigation found no problem.

A third reason Timothy could be courageous was that he had *the anointing and power of the Holy Spirit.* The Spirit would give him the power to speak before kings, governors, lawyers and nations without fear. Paul had experienced that power before the authorities and wanted to assure Timothy that the same power was available to him.

Added to all these reasons that Timothy could be courageous was the purpose for which he was called—to proclaim the Gospel, the message that "death has been swallowed up in victory. Where, O death, is your victory? Where, O death, is your sting?" (1 Corinthians 15:54–55). No other religion in the world can offer hope to humanity, proclaiming freedom for those bound and making all things new. Only those who know Jesus can look into the face of a brutal, cruel and cold death and say, "Where is your power? Where is your sting?" Through Christ we are more than conquerors in life and in death.

Because of these things, Timothy could go forward in courage. Because of these things, you and I can go forward in courage . . . and must.

What Is Courage?

But what is courage? How can we wrap our hands around it and bring it into our own lives? It is a word that has been used in countless plays, poems and speeches. One by which leaders have hoped to put to flight weak and hurting men, to stir up within them the sparks to keep the fire burning and hope alive. It's a word many in this world are familiar with, but few really know it by personal experience.

There is an element to courage that can only be understood when it is experienced at the moment of need, probably much like the moment when David stood before Goliath with stone and slingshot in trembling hand.

But there is another side of courage that I want to focus on, one by which it is defined: courage—"the *state or quality of mind or spirit* that enables one to face danger, fear, or vicissitudes with self-possession, confidence, and resolution; bravery."[2] Simply put, courage is the resolve in our spirit that we will stand strong no matter what comes. Our mind is made up—no difficulty will deter us. It is a determination that suffering cannot cause to quit. And it was an essential element to Timothy's ministry, as it is today with every servant of God.

When Paul encouraged Timothy to be unashamed and courageous, he was trying to prepare Timothy for all that lay ahead, to bring him to the place of decision where he determined once and for all that he would stand strong no matter what may come. This was also what Jesus did with His disciples in Luke 21:14–19, when He told them what would happen after He was gone. He, too, spoke of courage, telling them to *"make up your mind* not to worry beforehand how you will defend yourselves. For I will give you words and wisdom that none of your adversaries will be able to resist or contradict. . . . By standing firm you will gain life" (emphasis mine).

Again, these examples show us that courage is having a mind to suffer. It is counting the cost and moving forward though the price may be high. As G.K. Chesterton said, "Courage is almost a contradiction in terms. It means a strong desire to live taking the form of a readiness to die." It was that same kind of readiness that we read was in Caleb in Numbers 13.

Caleb and Joshua, along with 10 others, were sent to spy out the Promised Land. As they did, they saw it was a land filled with giants, but also a good land. So they brought back word to the people, saying, "Let us go up at once and take possession, for we are well able to overcome it" (Numbers 13:30, NKJV). But the other 10 men, gripped with fear, gave a different report, one of doom, gloom and defeat. The children of Israel believed their report and refused to enter the Promised Land. Only Caleb and Joshua did. Why? Because, as God said, "My servant Caleb . . . has a different spirit in him" (Numbers 14:24, NKJV). It was a spirit of courage, and because of that he was brought into the Promised Land while the others were left outside.

Let me ask you, do you have a different spirit in you, one that takes courage in God and braves the storms? Let each one of us make up our minds today that whatever comes in this nation, whatever opposition we face in our preaching of the Gospel, we will have the same resolve of courage that nothing can deter us from fighting the good fight, keeping the faith and winning the prize. Let us believe like David, Caleb and Paul that God is able to do the impossible and therefore press forward with hope.

Narayan Sharma, our leader from Nepal, spoke about a time when he was arrested for preaching the Gospel and had to go before the judge. He never said, "My wife and family are going to be without me. Please do something!" What he did say to me was, "You know, Uncle, maybe I will end up in prison for three years, but I want you to know I will have no regrets. I will have the best time sitting there reading and praying. I will be an example for the Church, and through my imprisonment, maybe something good will happen for my country." He had his mind made up—he would not turn back in the face of his trial.

It must be the same with us. I encourage you, therefore, to stay on your course. You are called to be a teacher, a leader, a husband, a wife—someone responsible for others and for God's work. There will be times when opposition will be very severe. In fact, the days are coming, I feel, in which we will face some incredible tempests of persecution. We must make up our minds now, knowing who has called us and realizing that without courage, no great thing has ever been accomplished. That which is worth winning always comes with a fight and with suffering, and to endure to the end we must be people of courage.

Courage Is a Choice

But courage is not just mental assent. There comes a time when that inner decision and conviction must be lived out in the moment of trial. Look throughout the Bible and you'll find numerous men and women who were full of courage and who did seemingly impossible things in their lifetime. From Esther risking her life for the justice of her people to Moses defying Pharaoh for the freedom of the children of God, story after story give witness to average men and women who lived courageous lives. But there is a connecting element in each of their stories. They *acted* upon their courage.

It is true that Caleb had a different spirit in him, one that was ready to defeat the giants in the Promised Land. That courageous spirit was necessary. But so was the very real battle of taking the land. There came the time when Caleb had to choose to go in his courage, face those giants and fight.

Consider Joshua as another example. God had led the children of Israel out of 400 years of slavery in Egypt, and He had promised Moses that the land of Canaan was for them and for their children. When Moses died, God restated His promise to Joshua, the one who took Moses' place to lead the children of Israel into the Promised Land.

But as Joshua was about to possess the land flowing with milk and honey, the great walled city of Jericho stood in the way. When Joshua saw this, God reminded him, "I promised this land to you Myself. I will never change My promise. This land is yours" (paraphrase, see Joshua 1:6–7, 9). God cannot lie, and this promise was absolutely fixed, firm, signed and sealed.

But there was one catch. Joshua must not be afraid; he must be courageous. He must take Jericho. Three times in eight verses in a single chapter, God exhorted Joshua to be "strong and courageous" (see Joshua 1).

He had the promise of God. He knew God had called him. He knew God was on his side and would provide the power needed. Joshua only needed now to *choose* to step out in courage.

Paul was another who knew the reality of making this kind of choice. There was a weathering of time, experience and pain behind his plea for Timothy to be full of courage. Paul was a seasoned traveler in the work of God. He had been through a variety of situations and worked alongside a variety of people, both before coming to Christ as well as afterward. I think it would be safe to say he had been around the block. One scholar suggests that in today's world, Paul traveled the equivalent of well over 13,400 airline miles. And given the fact that travel in the ancient Roman world often led over rough, rugged, primitive paths, this was no small task. Add on top of that the fact that Paul traveled through lands with the awareness that bandits were likely to meet him at any given time . . . and did! Read how he portrays his travels in 2 Corinthians 11:24–27:

> Five times I received from the Jews the forty lashes minus one. Three times I was beaten with rods, once I was stoned, three times I was shipwrecked, I spent a night and a day in the open sea, I have been constantly on the move. I have been in danger from rivers, in danger from bandits, in danger from my own countrymen, in danger from Gentiles; in danger in the city, in danger in the country, in danger at sea; and in danger from false brothers. I have labored and toiled and have often gone without sleep; I have known hunger and thirst and have often gone without food; I have been cold and naked.

Over and over and over again, Paul was "in danger," yet he never turned away from the Gospel or the call of God on his life. He continually made the choice to press on and stand courageous. Timothy must follow in his footsteps and do the same.

Paul's plea for Timothy to be different in this regard was not just a shallow suggestion. Throughout his years of ministry,

Paul saw many who chose the opposite, bowing to the pressure of suffering and shame and turning away rather than standing strong. In 2 Timothy 1:15, Paul says, "You know that everyone in the province of Asia has deserted me, including Phygelus and Hermogenes."

The Greek word used in verse 15 for "turned away" denotes that a specific event had taken place that caused many people to forsake the faith. As seen in Acts 19, Paul had traveled to Ephesus and preached the Gospel. "This went on for two years, so that all the Jews and Greeks who lived in the province of Asia heard the word of the Lord" (Acts 19:10). But not too long after that, persecution broke out and Paul was rearrested. Once that happened, many people who claimed to be servants of God where Timothy was located turned away from the faith, denying Paul and Christ. Timothy couldn't be like this. He must be different. Paul was warning him, "But for you, Timothy, don't retreat. Don't go back." Timothy's courage was crucial. Like Paul, he must be willing to be a "fool for Christ's sake" (1 Corinthians 4:10, NKJV).

You, too, must be willing to be a fool for Christ's sake. You, too, must make the choice to be courageous and not turn away or back down. Nepal shall be saved. India shall be saved. Bhutan shall be saved. Bangladesh shall be saved. Myanmar shall be saved. Tibet shall be saved. Sri Lanka shall be saved. God says, "I want you to be courageous. Don't let fear or intimidation creep into your heart. If it does, My promise will never come to pass."

What will happen in the days to come in our own nation? Missionary Staines and his two young boys were burned to death in Orissa. Hundreds of churches have been burned down in many parts of the country. It is common for us to hear every week that some of our brothers have been beaten. It is not unusual to hear that during Sunday morning worship some anti-Christian group has disturbed a service and beaten up the believers.

This is a time, then, that Paul's message to Timothy is especially relevant for us. Will things get easier in the days to come? We can hope so, but it is possible that they will not. Regardless, we must keep pressing forward.

You Cannot Kill Such a Man!

In the early days of my serving the Lord, I traveled with a team to Rajasthan. Six teams had gone before us to a particular town, and each was beaten and chased out. Some brothers were so badly beaten that they could not even stand on their legs.

We had the hopes that our team would be different—it was not. Upon our arrival, we were severely beaten and our Bibles were burned. After that, one of the men who beat us up brought a large can of black, murky engine oil and said, "We have brought this to pour over you and your vehicle and burn you all alive." If it weren't for another man who said, "Wait, give them five minutes to leave this place. If they don't go, then we will kill them," we would not be alive today. Hurriedly, we dragged ourselves into our truck, weak and bloody, and escaped. We never went back to that place. Many years had gone by, and not once had I heard of any ministry going on in that town.

Then one day I got news that a very young man who had just finished Bible college felt the Lord calling him to plant a church in this village. His leaders thought he was out of his mind to even consider this mission field. But the young man felt God was calling him there so the leaders gathered around and prayed for him. This young man's courage reminds me of Acts 20, when Paul, knowing the persecution that awaited him and with many people pleading for him not to go, still pressed forward to fulfill the call God had given him.

The young brother did face a tremendous amount of persecution, and death threats were made on his life from the anti-Christian elements. Finally, he was given an ultimatum: stop preaching or be killed. The way this young man responded reflects the courage he had in his God. He told those who opposed him that he came there to die, that, like Paul, his life meant nothing to him, if only he could finish the race the Lord Jesus had called him to (see Acts 20:24). He would not stop preaching.

The end result? With much difficulty, a church was planted in that village, and many now gather there to worship the Lord! I was invited to dedicate the church building, and I never will forget the testimony of that brother who was willing to risk his life to declare, "Jesus is Lord!"

You see, you cannot kill a man who is already dead. The men who persecuted that young man saw his boldness and courage and could not figure out what on earth he was all about, just as the rulers and elders who "saw the courage of Peter and John . . . were astonished and . . . took note that these men had been with Jesus" (Acts 4:13).

That is the key—to not be ashamed of the Gospel because it is the power of God for salvation and to courageously risk our lives to see this Gospel preached in all the world.

That does not mean you should go out accusing, fighting and getting arrested in foolishness. Even Jesus often found a way out when He was about to get into trouble with the authorities. He did not give Himself over to them before it was His time. But He still went about His Father's business with courage.

In the early days of God's work in Myanmar, when a missionary was caught and beaten for preaching the Gospel, he would tell the authorities that if they released him he would agree to leave the village. But the local authorities knew better, responding, "Do you think we are that stupid? We see the marks and bruises on your body, and your courage and willingness to suffer for your faith and your God. We know that all our people will get converted to your God if we let you go. We will not let you go."

Our courage speaks loud, testifying to the truth of the Gospel. Let us reconcile today that we are dead, that we live for a higher call, and in that courageously go about the work our Lord has called us to.

"I Know Whom I Have Believed . . ."

In 2 Timothy 1:8, Paul tells young Timothy to *"join with me* in suffering for the gospel" (emphasis mine). Once again, Paul's life has paved the way and sets the example for Timothy. And what an example it was! Read through the book of Acts, and you'll see just a glimpse of the kind of situations Paul encountered and the kind of courage he faced each one with, often running right back to the very towns in which he was just beaten and left for dead.

What was the keeping power behind Paul's courage? How was he able to stand up again and again in the face of all the opposition that came his way? How could he confidently plead with Timothy to stand in that same kind of courage? The answer is found in 2 Timothy 1:12, where Paul says, "I know whom I have believed, and am convinced that he is able to guard what I have entrusted to him for that day."

Paul found his courage in knowing the Lord who said, "All authority has been given to Me. The gates of hell will not prevail against My Church. No one can stand against you when I am with you." The secret to doing great exploits courageously for the Lord is our understanding of our God. Paul knew God. He knew that He alone was sovereign and in control of every circumstance. He knew that God works all things together for the good of those who love Him and who are called according to His purpose (see Romans 8:28). His hope was in Him. His courage was in Him.

Listen to Paul as he stands upon the broken deck of a shipwrecked boat, proclaiming to a crew of fearful men expecting their soon death. As they're tossing barrels and cargo aside in hopes for a few more moments to live, Paul stands up and says, "I urge you to keep up your courage, because not one of you will be lost; only the ship will be destroyed. Last night an angel *of the God whose I am and whom I serve* stood beside me and said, 'Do not be afraid' " (Acts 27:22–24, emphasis mine). Paul knew to whom he belonged, whom he believed and that He was faithful and strong and sovereign.

Even while sitting in prison, Paul maintained this attitude. Emperor Nero may have thought, *This Paul is my prisoner. He's finished.* But Paul was declaring, "I am not Nero's prisoner. I am the Lord's prisoner. The Lord is my Master, and because I am His, I am free even in prison." Paul knew his God, and it affected the way he saw every situation in his life and it determined his courage.

We must have this same confidence. We must hear the One who called us saying, "Fear not, for I have redeemed you; I have called you by your name; you are Mine. When you pass through the waters, I will be with you; and through the rivers, they shall not overflow you. When you walk through the fire, you shall not be burned, nor shall the flame scorch you. For I am the LORD your God" (Isaiah 43:1–3, NKJV). In this we must take courage and stand strong, going forth to possess the land He has promised to us.

Encouragement from the Lord

My brothers and sisters, God has given you responsible positions in His kingdom. None of us, in ourselves, has the courage to face difficulty and opposition. None of us wants to face misunderstanding and accusation or loneliness and loss. But God can make our hearts strong and courageous to stand up under any trial.

God has given us many opportunities. Through radio, television, literature and many young missionaries, He has opened doors that no man can shut. The way things are happening, this nation will be a nation where on top of every hill, below in every valley and inside every hut, the cross will be raised up and we will hear Jesus Christ being worshiped!

Let us therefore take courage in our God and see these things come to pass. And when the battle gets rough as it is sometimes bound to do, lift up your eyes and see Him, just as Stephen, when he was being persecuted, "gazed into heaven and saw the glory of God, and Jesus" (Acts 7:55, NKJV). Our God is good, and He knows we are in a battle. He is the Good Shepherd who takes care of us, never leaving us alone or without some kind of encouragement. There is always a Jonathan for David, a widow for Elijah. Take confidence in His care and stand strong.

I want to be a believer who does not live with fear but with courage. The days to come are the best days, and we need the courage to see that we are on the winning team. We *are* winning—not with cleverness, money or power, but by the power of the Holy Spirit and with Jesus the Conqueror going before us. *He* is our reason for being courageous.

You were born for such a time as this. Be bold as a lion!

seven

total dependence
on the Lord

Dependence on the Lord alone is central to our lives as we live for and serve God. Our attitude must always reflect the belief that God is our only source—not information, evaluation and judgments from culture, someone else's views or our own prejudices. This concept, if we understand it, is very simple but profound.

Why is this so important? Jeremiah 17:5–8 tells us, serving as a much-needed reminder for today—

Cursed is the one who trusts in man, who depends on flesh for his strength and whose heart turns away from the LORD. He will be like a bush in the wastelands; he will not see prosperity when it comes. He will dwell in the parched places of the desert, in a salt land where no one lives. But blessed is the man who trusts in the LORD, whose confidence is in him. He will be like a tree planted by the water that sends out its roots by the stream. It does not fear when heat comes; its leaves are always green. It has no worries in a year of drought and never fails to bear fruit.

There are two key areas of our lives that automatically show whether or not we truly have the heart attitude of depending upon the Lord. One area is in *how we deal with the difficulties of life.*

Many times our natural response to any difficulty, challenge or task tends first to be, "What must *I* do to get this done?" We look inward to ourselves or outward to friends, family or doctors. Most of us do not naturally think, *I have a headache; I need to talk to the Lord about this. The Lord is my Healer.* Or, *I need money. The Lord is my source. I will ask Him.* Rather, when we get a headache, the first thing we think is, *Where is the aspirin?* When we get sick, our first thought tends to be, *Where is the nearest doctor?* When a problem comes, the first thing we think is, *I must contact headquarters.* When we need money, our first response is, *I must call the office immediately.* These things are not necessarily bad in and of themselves. It is when our dependence is upon them rather than on God that we begin to walk on shaky ground.

Second Chronicles 16:12–13 records a fascinating and sobering warning in this regard:

> In the thirty-ninth year of his reign Asa was afflicted with a disease in his feet. Though his disease was severe, even in his illness he did not seek help from the LORD, but only from the physicians. Then in the forty-first year of his reign Asa died and rested with his fathers.

Do you see what happened? For 39 years, God helped Asa as king and blessed him. As Asa sought God's face, God was gracious to him and helped him all throughout his journey.

But after a while, Asa's dependence began to drift from the Lord. So much so that when he developed a disease in his feet he did not seek God for a solution. Instead, he sought out all the physicians.

Was it wrong for Asa to go to the doctors? Did he make a mistake by taking medicine? No, seeking medical help is not the issue. The issue is that over the years Asa had become self-confident, arrogant and proud of all the doctors, money and infrastructure he had in his kingdom and put his trust in the things he had established as king. I believe he got sick for a reason: His heart had grown cold and departed from the Lord. He had grown dependent on his army, his money and his people. God allowed the sickness as a means to wake him up, saying, *Come and seek My face. Come to Me. Talk to Me. I am your Healer.* But Asa would not.

What a sad account. My brothers and sisters, let us stay dependent on God and never place anything before or above Him.

Another area that shows where our dependence lies is in *how we handle the ministry to which the Lord has called us.* We may enjoy good organization, good leaders, good education and wonderful resources to get the job done. But none of that has anything to do with the authentic work of God if our dependence is not on Him.

A servant of God can be tempted to use his money, power, influence, connections or authority to solve his problems and get the job done. That, however, is a picture of hell. He is borrowing strength from the position God has given him and attacking God's work. Instead of fasting for the ministry and problems that arise, instead of seeking God's face, he relies on his position or title and uses it to force a solution.

What kind of worker are you? Are you always falling back on the arm of flesh? Do you depend on your own energy and strength? Remember, serving God is not a matter of being crafty and smart. In fact, it is usually those who are clever who do not last very long in the ministry because they allow God no place in their lives.

It is because of this truth that my prayer to God is continually, *Let me be like a little child. Let me make mistakes. But please, let me not be clever in doing Your work.*

The Lord resides with the lowly and humble, with those who will depend upon Him and give glory to Him—not with the strong who know all the answers and how to get the job done.

Our attitude about ministry accomplishments reveals where our dependence truly lies. When God uses us for His glory, we can easily start to think, "I did it! I am gifted! I am talented! It is my position, my decisions and my ingenuity that got it done! I am the one who . . ." We forget that we are but dust, "jars of clay" as Scripture says (see 2 Corinthians 4:7). Yet within these jars of clay is a great treasure—the glory and power of the living God! But we must remember we are merely the vessels, and even in that, just clay vessels, not gold, silver, bronze or even steel.

Do you recognize this? Just because God has given you responsibilities and opportunities to serve others does not mean you are a gold vessel. In yourself you have no value. You are an earthen vessel, and what that vessel contains belongs not to you, but to the Lord who committed it to you. All is from Him, for Him, through Him and for His glory so that the glory may not be in the jar itself, but in the Lord!

Imagine how absurd it would have been if the disciples, after feeding the 5,000, boasted in themselves at the miracle that took place. They were merely distributors, going around with the baskets and giving out from the abundance of food that God had provided (see Mark 6:33–44). Who got the glory?

Not the ones who distributed, but the One who provided.

We, too, are distributors. But in Christendom today we tend to parade the clever people—the healers and miracle-workers with big names—as if they are the source. How sad! How far we have fallen from being godly in our thinking!

All of us would be nothing—just earthen vessels with nothing in them—if the Lord had not filled us with the gold and silver of His plan, purpose and work. And if God allowed us to be sick and lying in a hospital somewhere, it would not take long to find out how fragile we really are.

I pray that among us, our attitude toward the ministry and our responsibilities as servants of God will be one that in all things we will look to God alone as our source, continually living lives that recognize who we are, and stay dependent on Him.

We're All the Same in Christ

The apostle Paul. Born into a rich, prestigious family. Taught at the finest academic school under the most acclaimed instructors. Earned a Ph.D. from the best university of his day. Accepted as a member of the prominent Sanhedrin, the ruling council of his nation. Strong temperament and ability. Type-A personality, born to be a leader. Philosopher. Thinker. Theologian.

With a track record like this, why does Paul tell Timothy, "You then, my son, *be strong in the grace that is in Christ Jesus*" (2 Timothy 2:1, emphasis mine)? Of all that Paul could be strong in, why does he not boast in anything he has in himself? Consider what he says in Philippians 3:4–6: "If anyone else thinks he has reasons to put confidence in the flesh, I have more: circumcised on the eighth day, of the people of Israel, of the tribe of Benjamin, a Hebrew of Hebrews; in regard to the law, a Pharisee; as for zeal, persecuting the church; as for legalistic righteousness, faultless."

But he doesn't boast in himself. In fact, he says that "whatever was to my profit I now consider loss for the sake of Christ" (Philippians 3:7).

Why doesn't Paul boast? Because he knew that in order to live a life pleasing to the Lord it must be a life of total dependence on Him. It is this kind of attitude in ministry that keeps us on a healthy course, honoring God and producing fruit that lasts.

On the other hand, Timothy was the complete opposite—in temperament and in every other way—from Paul. He was young, sick and weak. His family background was messed up—a Jewish mother and a Gentile father. It was as if he were from the low caste. The Greeks said he was a betrayer, and the Jewish people said he was nothing but a dog. But Paul thought Timothy's background was wonderful! Why? Because Timothy knew he was of the least and the lowest, he had nothing of himself to boast in. God could easily use him to bring all the glory to Himself.

In Philippians 3, Paul sums it up for Timothy saying, "All that I was, all that I knew, everything that I once held as important, it all meant nothing. It didn't work or make me a more useful servant of God. For several years I sat alone wondering what to do with my life. Then the Lord said to me, 'Paul, I want to use you, but you must give up all these things and become a zero.' So I decided to take all my degrees, all my wonderful background, all my abilities, all my skills, talents and temperament, and call them cow dung."

Have you ever seen people hang their university or college degrees on their wall? Would someone ever do the same with cow dung—dry it, frame it and write his name under it? No, but that's exactly what Paul did. The high priest and other leaders and theologians had their degrees hanging on their walls, but if you had walked into Paul's office, you would have found him sitting there scribbling away, his degree of cow dung hanging above him on the wall. Who would honor him with that as his qualification?

Paul recognized that in him dwelled "nothing good" (Romans 7:18). He knew Timothy was blessed because he did not have to go through the same mess of having much and then having to throw it all away. Paul knew how important it is to be careful about living life dependent on nothing and no one but the Lord.

You see, in Christ we are all the same. If you started out with nothing like Timothy or were considered something like Paul, either way it has no merit. We must all start from zero "to show that this all-surpassing power is from God and not from us" (2 Corinthians 4:7).

We must live in the awareness of this truth and recognize that God is our source, depending on Him alone and not on anything of ourselves. Every time I sit before the studio microphone to record a radio broadcast, I remind myself that I represent my Lord and that He is the One using me to speak on His behalf. It is not me doing it. I must keep in mind that my hand is His hand and my tongue is His tongue and that His resources allow me to represent Him. What a difference in thinking!

The Battle for Our Dependence

We must be wise and recognize that there is a very real battle for our dependence. The enemy knows that if he can turn our eyes and trust off of the Lord, he will have a mighty foothold into our lives and ministry and will be able to tear both down.

Why did David come under God's curse and the nation

of Israel have to face God's judgment? Because "Satan rose up against Israel and incited David to take a census of Israel" (1 Chronicles 21:1). Notice that it was the devil who planted the thought in David's mind to number his army. I am sure David thought, *I must fight another war. I had better be sure about what I have available to me.* It probably seemed like a good suggestion, but it was a tool of the enemy to destroy David's ministry as he began to look to the strength and number of his army rather than to the strength and power of God.

How true it is that "our struggle is not against flesh and blood, but against the rulers, against the authorities, against the powers of this dark world and against the spiritual forces of evil in the heavenly realms" (Ephesians 6:12). David's dependence on the Lord was diluted, and it not only affected his own life, but the whole nation of Israel. How crucial it is that we depend on the Lord!

This same battle for dependence was what Jesus also faced out in the wilderness in Matthew 4. Three times Satan tempted Him to take His eyes off of the Father and look to the physical things around Him—bread for His hungry stomach, a quick, false way to victory and ease from the battle. And three times, Jesus remembered the Father, His words and promises, depended on His strength and came out victorious.

We must respond to the attacks of the enemy in the same way and not give him a foothold into our lives by turning our eyes and trust off of the Lord. When we have problems with sickness, bitterness and anguish in our families or ministries, let us respond rooted in the promises of God, knowing He is faithful. May our hearts continually look to our God to meet every need we may ever have, then when the temptations of the enemy come we will be able to defeat him, turn away from his thoughts and look to our God, trusting in Him.

Spiritual Midlife Crisis

It is a mystery to me, but it seems that around 40 years of age, the man who appears to be spiritual, burdened for the lost world and serving God without concern for money or esteem becomes unbroken, independent, stiff-necked and proud in the secret world of his inner life. He is like a little worm that finally breaks free of the cocoon and comes out with all its true colors. The secret world of his heart comes to light in a kind of midlife crisis in the spiritual realm. Until this time, he was able to control outward behavior by copying humility in others, but the true nature that was sleeping inside wakes up.

This seems to be how it is: When someone is first called into the ministry, his attitude is, "I don't have the ability or skill. I am a nobody, and I don't know why God chose me to serve Him." This person says with Paul, "When I am weak, then I am strong." His ministry is powerful and his life bears witness to the mercy and goodness of God.

In the second phase of his ministry, often because of his humility, he is put into a leadership position. By then, he may have gotten an education and developed the skills that the Lord gave him. He is able to accomplish much for the kingdom because God honors a person who is broken and humble before Him.

In the third phase of his ministry, he is amazed at what he can do on behalf of the Lord. "Wow! I can't believe it. I prayed and this couple got a child after 14 years! This man was dying of cancer, but I prayed and he got up! I preached, and I can't believe that 300 people wept and came forward to receive the Lord! The training center barely had 100 students, but now we have 400!"

By the fourth phase, this individual draws confidence from himself and begins to boast in all that his life has accomplished. He begins to think he is really something and soon becomes a hindrance to the ministry. Why? Because the Holy Spirit walks away from him saying, "I can't work with a self-confident, stubborn individual." God resists the proud person (see James 4:6; 1 Peter 5:5).

On the outside it may appear that nothing has changed and that everything is good. He still preaches, he still prays and people still come to Christ, because God does not take back the gifting He gives. The individual deceives himself and thinks, "See, I prayed for that sick man who was dying and he got up. God is with me." But in reality he has become a stumbling block, keeping others from understanding God's grace. No longer is he pointing people to Jesus; instead, he is gathering disciples around himself. He changes colors according to the demand of the environment, like the survival technique of a chameleon.

The final phase of this man if he does not repent and turn back to dependence upon the Lord is that he will die with deep regrets. A classic example of this process is found in the life of Uzziah.

Uzziah was 16 years old and scared to death when the Lord called him to be king of Judah. Because of this, Uzziah sought God, and as a result, God strengthened his hand and made him a powerful king. Second Chronicles 26:5 says, "As long as he sought the LORD, God gave him success." And success he had as he defeated many undefeatable foes and became a blessing to those he led.

But sadly, later in his life we learn that "after Uzziah became powerful, his pride led to his downfall" (2 Chronicles 26:16). His dependence on the Lord diminished, and he actually usurped the role of the priests in the temple. When he did this, God allowed him to become leprous.

As is often the case when we take our dependence off of the Lord, Uzziah's blessings became his curse. His strength led to his destruction.

Was it wrong to have sat on the throne? Was it wrong to have been king? Was it wrong to have a million people following him? No. But Uzziah's dependence had shifted away from the Lord, who had given everything to him, and onto himself. And because of this, he was destroyed.

The Lord says, "No flesh shall glory in My presence" (paraphrase, see 1 Corinthians 1:27–29). God will make sure that everything built by flesh will be destroyed. That is what happened with Uzziah, Nebuchadnezzar, Solomon and millions of others. I don't want such destruction to be part of our lives or fellowship.

A Warning to Repent

What is the sign that a worker is no longer depending on the Lord and broken before God? It is his attitude.

Years ago, I used to murmur about recording my radio broadcast. My life was getting painful because of lack of time, and privately I said to Gisela, "I am so sick and tired. I can't do my radio broadcast anymore. I get up so early in the morning and then I work all day. I am emotionally drained. I wish somebody else would do it."

Then she said to me, "May I tell you something? You've been complaining about how important you are, how little time you have and how hard this job is. If you say it a few more times, God will remove you and put somebody else in charge who is better than you. Don't you understand? When you heard God's call to lead Gospel for Asia, you gave up your teaching and preaching ministry and complained that your gift was not to live in America and teach people about missions. But how can you forget that God, in His mercy, gave you a microphone and a world to speak to? God has a thousand people waiting in queue for one opportunity to do a better job than you are doing. But God still shows you mercy. Be careful. The work is not something to boast about or to complain about, but rather our privilege."

If you are serving the Lord with the wrong attitude, would you please receive this warning and repent?

In the short time of our ministry, because our growth has been so fast, I have seen God empower the young and helpless with His might and do great things through them to reach the lost. At the same time, I have watched many people, who started well and depending on the Lord, fall by the wayside because they began to boast in themselves, and their hearts grew proud. I cry over these things, knowing that Satan has us as one of his targets, seeking to tear us down and take us out of ministry by making our hearts proud, just like Uzziah and Asa.

I encourage you to please ask the Lord to search your heart to see if there is anything there that may be leading you down this destructive road of depending on yourself and external things rather than on God. Ask yourself the following questions:

- Do I believe God for the results of my ministry?
- When there is success in my ministry, do I have an absolute awareness that it happened because I trusted the Lord?
- Do I fast and pray, waiting on God for my ministry to succeed?
- Do I ask the Lord for the money I need for tracts, books, food and train tickets?
- Do I have ownership of and a burden for my ministry?

If you answered *no* to some of these questions, please repent. People who work with you and look up to you may be destroyed by your arrogance and pride if you do not change your dependence back to the Lord. When God gives you the opportunity to repent and change, please do not ignore Him. Humble yourself before God, and He will restore you.

You and I Are Clay Pots

Let us become like Gideon in Judges 7. When God called him to defeat the Midianites, he was weak and scared. When God said, "Don't worry about the Midianites," Gideon replied, "But God, what do You mean, 'Don't worry about them'? Don't You see there are hundreds of thousands of Midianites out there, and I have only 32,000 men to fight them?"

"Yes, Gideon, I see them too. I have better eyesight than you. But Gideon, can't you see Me?"

"Yes, but You are sitting up there and I am here. You know I'm not a strong man. I don't have anything in me that qualifies me to lead these people. Plus my family background is the least and the lowest. I have no money, no experience—nothing. Yet You say, 'No problem.' You may be able to say that, but this is a problem for me."

"Gideon, listen. Those 32,000 people you have—they are too many. If you keep those 32,000 men, when the victory is won, they will say, 'It is by our might and strength. We did it.' I don't want that. So tell all those who are scared to go home."

Ten thousand remained, and God told Gideon to tell all those who knelt down by the water to drink to go home. Now only 300 remained. And God said, "Perfect!"

If I had been in Gideon's shoes, I would have said, "God, I have fewer than one percent of the people I had! How in the world are we supposed to defeat the greatest, largest army with 300 people?"

But as is always the case, God's plan is perfect. And He had a plan for Gideon and his 300 men—each would carry clay pots with candles in them and at night head for the enemy's camp. When the time was right, the men were to break their clay pots.

They followed the Lord's instruction, and the sound of the pots breaking and the myriads of lights frightened their enemy so much that it sent them fleeing. That night, Gideon and his men defeated their foe by the Lord's strength and might.

And so it must be with us. God has a plan for our lives and ministry, one that is not accomplished by might or by power, but by His Spirit and dependence on Him. Just like Gideon and his army, when these earthen vessels are broken from depending upon ourselves, the treasure within us is able to shine forth and bring glory to God. Remember that!

That is just like Jesus, isn't it? He Himself said, "I am broken. This is My body that is broken for you." It is through brokenness and dependence on the Lord, not on ourselves, that we become useful people in God's kingdom.

How I hope we will have a testimony to the world and to the Church that we are a people walking with Him in total dependence, a people who are true servants simply serving the Lord and depending on His strength alone.

"Some trust in chariots and some in horses, but we trust in the name of the LORD our God" (Psalm 20:7). *Is this your confession as well?*

disciple maker

One of the first things Jesus did when He started His ministry on earth was to choose 12 men to give His time and energy to disciple. He lived with them, laughed with them and taught them day by day through the various situations of life. He intentionally invested His life in them, knowing that one day they would have to go and do the very same thing—teach what He had taught and bear witness to the truth. And when the day came that He said to them, "Go and make disciples of all nations, baptizing them in the name of the Father and of the Son and of the Holy Spirit, and teaching them to obey everything I have commanded" (Matthew 28:19–20), they went out and fulfilled His command.

This seems to be the manner in which the work of God continues through the generations. All throughout the Old Testament we see men of God discipling others. For every Elijah there was an Elisha being trained up; for every Moses there was a Joshua ready to step up to the call. And in the New Testament, Jesus continued this pattern of growth for the kingdom of God.

The apostle Paul knew the impact of personal discipleship

from early on. You see, Paul may not have been accepted by the disciples if it were not for Barnabas taking him under his care and discipling him. For more than a year, Barnabas invested his life into Paul as together they worked side by side teaching the church at Antioch. Read through Acts 9–15, and you'll find "Barnabas and Paul" mentioned numerous times.

Paul continued this pattern by discipling Timothy, pouring his years, tears and teaching into him. Now, as Paul's days drew to a close, he reminds Timothy he must do the same—"The things you have heard me say in the presence of many witnesses entrust to reliable men who will also be qualified to teach others" (2 Timothy 2:2).

And so it must be among us. Mature brothers and sisters must be disciple makers all the time, seeking out those whom they can care for and train in the ways of God. Every mature believer must be a disciple maker, aiding in the spiritual growth of those younger in the Lord, for this is the way the kingdom of God is built and continues on.

In fact, to build up others must be our fundamental attitude in the ministry. Without it, no fulfillment of the Great Commission is possible. The Great Commission is not just about preaching and distributing Gospel tracts—it is the act of *discipling and teaching,* a process of maturity that occurs as we pour our lives into another.

The Importance of Discipleship

Unfortunately, in the Christian world today, the need for discipleship is great. There are many who receive teaching and hear sermon after sermon, but few who really have someone discipling them. This is because true disciplers are too few.

Many may be considered disciplers because of the degrees they possess, but that means nothing if their lives are not paving the way for a younger brother to follow. It is our lives that make the difference, not our knowledge. Anyone can say, "Young brother, you must spend an hour in prayer and meditate on the Scripture," but the young brother will not do it if he does not see his teacher doing it. Our teaching about evangelism and leading people to Christ is compromised if we teach it only as a doctrine or classroom subject, never giving out Gospel tracts or taking opportunities to lead others to Christ. Our life must bear witness to these principles, and we must become the example for a younger brother to follow and grow in the Lord. This is true discipleship.

I was shocked once when I was visiting a student in Calcutta working toward a Master's degree in Theology. As we sipped tea, I watched the crowds flowing through the street like a river. There were literally thousands of people, most who probably never had heard the Gospel. I said to the young man, "Why don't we do some tract distribution?"

"Sorry," he said, "there are no tracts. Nobody has tracts here."

Then I asked him, "How long have you been here?"

"Two and a half years."

"Have you ever witnessed to anyone, led anyone to Christ during this entire time?"

He replied, "No."

May the Lord have mercy on this young man! He may be brilliant and have a degree after his name, but he became a backslidden, heartless, spiritless reprobate who used God's money to get an education, only to become a servant of God with no heart for God or the lost. His life should have been producing great fruit and serving as an example for younger brothers to follow, but it was not. How tragic!

We are responsible for the good measure the Lord has poured into our lives, responsible to pass it on to a younger brother and see him grow up to be a man of God who goes out and in turn makes disciples. We cannot simply accrue all of our spiritual knowledge for our own sake—it is to be given out, used to encourage, edify and build up the family of God.

Are you a disciple maker? Do you have one, two or three people you are training in the ways of God? If not, pray and ask the Lord to make you a disciple maker like He was and then show you who He wants you to invest your life in.

How Jesus Trained His Disciples

The four Gospels present Jesus in action training His disciples. Because Jesus is our ultimate model, I want to emphasize six particular aspects of the way He made disciples, which we would do well to follow as we invest our lives into discipling others.

Those He discipled were teachable. All those Jesus selected (except Judas) were normal, simple, working people. Peter, John and James were fishermen—rough characters, unrefined. But Jesus selected them, seeing past their stony exteriors, because they had hearts that were willing to learn. Deep inside they were teachable.

Godly leaders are not made with money or education. They are made by transferring values from a godly older person to a younger person who may not be godly now, but who is willing to learn the ways of God. If a person has a hard heart and is unwilling to learn, there is no reason to try to disciple them. That is why Jesus chose only the teachable to be His disciples.

He lived with them. For three and a half years, Jesus stayed with His disciples. He spent day after day with them. He was not only their Teacher but also the subject they were studying. He was their school. His life taught them.

Can you teach from your own life, as Jesus did, and say,

"Follow me"? Can you honestly say to your younger brother, as Paul said in 1 Corinthians 11:1, "Follow my example, as I follow the example of Christ"? When was the last time you led someone to Christ or gave out a Gospel tract, so that today you can witness to a younger brother about the joy it was to do those things?

Are there one or two brothers who come to your house regularly to spend time with you and your family? Do they know how you live and what your weaknesses are? Do they know about the times you have had to repent to your wife and kids, or are you keeping the door shut? No worker is truly God's worker who cannot expose his life to others whom he is trying to help. Let your life teach others what it means to truly walk with Christ.

He required absolute obedience. His disciples had to count the cost of consecration. Hundreds of people wanted to follow Jesus, but few understood that meant forsaking their own will for His. It was a path of absolute obedience.

Following Christ is not a light thing. Jesus was more concerned with gathering a few committed individuals who would obey Him no matter what, rather than many who were half-hearted.

One particular passage of Scripture strengthens this fact. Once to a whole group of people, Jesus said, "Unless you eat the flesh of the Son of Man and drink his blood, you have no life in you" (John 6:53). The people responded, "That is a hard saying," and many turned away (see John 6:60, 66). Easy as that, their discipleship was finished!

If I had been Jesus, I would have explained this saying more, but He did not. I might have said, "Look, fellows, I am not talking about My actual flesh and blood. I am explaining about the sacrifice and commitment you must make, forgetting all and following Me." But He didn't do that. Why not?

Because He didn't want the superficial and self-seeking following Him. The person who is following Christ for position, power, money, excitement or something to do will never follow Him in absolute obedience, which is what He required. They must be willing to walk as He walked, obedient to the Father, even unto death.

In his book *The Master Plan of Evangelism,* Dr. Robert E. Coleman writes about this, saying,

> Jesus was making men to lead his church to conquest, and no one can ever be a leader until first he has learned to follow a leader. So he brought up his future commanders from the ranks, drilling in them along the way the necessity for discipline and respect for authority. There could be no insubordination in His command. No one knew better than Jesus that the satanic forces of darkness against them were well organized and equipped to make ineffectual any half-hearted effort of evangelism. They could not possibly outwit the devilish powers of this world unless they gave strict adherence to him who alone knew the strategy of victory. This required absolute obedience to the Master's will, even as it meant complete abandonment of their own. [1]

You are under authority. All of us are. Make sure that you, in turn, take a younger brother and help him walk with the Lord in the same commitment and absolute obedience to the Lord.

He completely gave of Himself. Jesus completely gave Himself to the disciples. He imparted everything He was to them, holding nothing back. He opened His life to them.

Jesus could have done the opposite—demanding He be treated as the king He really was and drawing a clear separation between the disciples and Himself. But He didn't do this.

And neither must we.

I have been very intentional in tearing down any kind of pyramid structure in the leadership of Gospel for Asia. This kind of structure is one in which there is one person at the top and everyone else under his feet, and that top person insists that everyone under him must obey him. I don't think that is the way Christ wanted it. In fact, He taught the opposite: "If anyone wants to be first, he must be the very last, and the servant of all" (Mark 9:35).

How do you become the servant of all? In your attitude and your behavior. You give of yourself. You go out of your way to help, encourage and pray for others. If you want to train somebody, don't sit at the top of the pyramid; rather, come to the other person's level. Be like Jesus—give yourself to the people around you, being an example of Christ and discipling them in this same way.

He showed the way. Christ worked wonderfully through demonstration. He did not say, "Get there on your own, and then you'll figure out what to do." No, He said, "Follow Me. I am the Way."

Jesus was the model. In John 15:12 He said, "My command is this: Love each other as I have loved you." For three and a half years He took care of His disciples, defended them, protected them, covered their sins and loved them. He did everything for them. And in the Upper Room, just before going to the cross, He said, "Children, come. I want to tell you something. This is My commandment: Love one another as I have loved you."

He showed them the way—and so must you as a discipler. Be godly and go out with younger brothers to minister. Pray with them, weep with them and show them the way. Conduct yourself so that when those you are discipling come to your house, they will find their teacher, the holy man of God, giving a bath to his son, getting the eggs from the chickens, sweeping the floor or out getting milk. Your student will think, *My teacher washes dishes? He makes tea? He gives baths to his little child? I never thought he would do things like that!* From these small actions you will have preached the most powerful sermons without a single word.

Train people by demonstrating and showing them the way. Let them see that the reason you did not answer the door on the first knock was because you were praying with your wife and kids as a family. Let them see that you were so burdened by someone going astray that your whole family fasted and prayed for that one. When you do that, they will say, "One day, when I am married and have children, I will pray with my family too. I want to show the world how a Christian family is supposed to be."

Instead of discussing and gossiping about others who are not acting as they should, let others see that you fast and pray for the Lord to help those people. Instead of just talking about seeking forgiveness from another, be the one who repents of your own sin toward the other person. If your daughter were asked if she wants to be like her mommy when she grows up, may she be able to say, "I would want to live forever if I could be just like my mommy! She is so gentle, loving, patient, forgiving and supportive of my daddy. She never complains or gossips about anyone. Her life is full of joy. I want to be just like my mommy."

The world must see how you live, serving as the example for those around you. Disciple like Jesus did—show the way through your life.

He delegated responsibility. In Matthew 10:5, we find Jesus sending out the disciples to do the things He had been doing— healing the sick, raising the dead, driving out demons and much more. He delegated the responsibility of the ministry into these disciples' hands.

To disciple and see growth, you, too, must delegate responsibility. Give others a job to do. Not only do they grow in their own walk with the Lord, but the ministry grows as well. It is amazing how much some of our brothers get done! How do they do it? They simply delegate.

Delegating means trusting others with jobs or duties. You might think, *Nobody is able to do this like me.* You are making a mistake. Remember that at some point somebody trusted you with responsibility. Were you perfect when you were given that responsibility? Didn't you make some mistakes? Release other people, then, to take some of your tasks and empower them by trusting them.

Gospel for Asia grew in a short time to become the organization it is today because it empowered people to take over new and increasing responsibilities.

Take Nepal as an example. Before the work started there, many Christian leaders told me horror stories, saying Nepal was the worst place in the whole world to go and that I should trust no one there. But I said, "Lord, You love Nepal. You want us to be there for Your purposes. You must have a man there who loves and trusts You, because You loved and trusted me."

Then I watched as God raised up Narayan Sharma, who has an impeccable testimony and a commitment to reach his people. As I began to work with him, I learned in a few short years of his genuineness, his godliness and his burden for his people. I told him, "Brother Narayan, you are not working for Gospel for Asia; I am working for you. Nepal is yours. I am your servant. You tell me what you want to do."

The work began to grow, the training center grew, the land was purchased and churches were started. I did not tell him a single thing to do. He told me what we must do and how I could be of help to him.

When I find a brother who is faithful to handle much, I give him much and say, "It's yours. Take it." I have nothing to fear because it is God's kingdom and God's call. So I let go. I don't want to control anything.

Remember that wherever you are, God trusted you to take responsibility. Your leaders trust you, and I, too, believe you can do it. In the same way, please entrust others with responsibility, with money and with people. If you find you are not trusting others, realize that it is because you are a controlling person and are insecure.

At the same time, it is not wrong to be cautious. The Bible warns against putting responsibility on anyone too quickly. It is good to supervise the person to whom you have delegated responsibility and set up some type of accountability. Mistakes may be made, but that too is a way in which we learn and grow. Being a disciple maker involves at its very essence, being like Jesus and, in turn, showing another how to be like Jesus. Pray and ask God to give you His patience and grace to train up others to follow Him.

Our Privilege

The making of disciples cannot be done solely by employing techniques of mass production. Disciples are not manufactured wholesale. They are produced one by one, with time, understanding and patience. May we recognize the great privilege the Lord gives us to raise up a new generation of believers who will do the will of God, and invest our lives in the brothers and sisters around us.

Make a difference. Be a disciple maker.

willing to suffer for His sake

The life of a civilian and the life of a soldier are worlds apart. The civilian is under no one's order. He can do as he pleases. From nine to five he can work at his job, earn his money, go to his home in the evening, enjoy his weekends and plan his vacations. He is a civilian.

But the soldier's life is different—he *is* under orders. He cannot simply do as he pleases.

If a soldier in Delhi gets a cable from his commanding officer that says, "Go to Cargill by this particular date," he must jump up and make plans immediately to get to Cargill. Despite how hard it may be to make a travel reservation, he knows he had better report to his post by the time he is expected. He leaves his family with the awareness that he may then be put on the front lines and might give his life there. But because he is a soldier, he responds to the call, leaving his own desires and life behind in order to fulfill the commitment he has made to his commanding officer, his nation and its security.

My brother, do you understand that you, too, are a soldier? My sister, do you realize that you have been enlisted? Do we realize the implications of this?

Paul understood very well what it meant to be a soldier. The Roman soldiers surrounding him in prison lived away from their homes and suffered for their cause. They paid the price. Their loyalty to their country and king was proven true by the way they suffered for it.

And we see from Paul's life that he also understood suffering and paid the price, his own body marked with the wounds of preaching the Gospel: "I bear on my body the marks of Jesus" (Galatians 6:17). Similar to the Roman soldiers guarding him in prison, Paul's loyalty to Christ was proven true by the suffering he endured. The book of 2 Corinthians is filled with Paul's anguish, pain and inconveniences. His life consisted of shipwrecks, nakedness, beatings, stonings, misunderstandings, desertion and being left to die. The pressure, tension and anguish were so great that in 2 Corinthians 1:8 (NKJV), he said, "We were burdened beyond measure, above strength, so that we despaired even of life." But it was these that Paul said gave proof that he belonged to Jesus (see Galatians 6:17). Paul's certificate of authenticity was not his accomplishments in the ministry, not the churches he planted or the revelations he had received, but rather his own personal commitment to inconvenience and his willingness to suffer.

Paul calls Timothy to this same acceptance of hardships, knowing that in the work of the Lord, suffering is bound to come. Timothy must be ready to endure this, and endure it as a good soldier (2 Timothy 2:3).

How is Timothy able to do this? Paul answers that question in 2 Timothy 2:4 (NKJV)—"No one engaged in warfare entangles himself with the affairs of this life, that he may please him who enlisted him as a soldier." If Timothy wanted to please the Lord as a good soldier, there was a price he must pay. He must conduct himself differently than those he lived among, keeping himself from getting tangled up in the affairs of this life. There would be things he must say "no" to, things he must go without, suffering he must endure. Why? Simply because he is a soldier.

And so it is with us. Our God has enlisted us for such a time as this to rescue the perishing. It is a very real battle for the souls of men that we are engaged in. We must not live with the mind-set that we are civilians. As soldiers, hardships will come—in many forms. Let us realize this price we are called to pay and count it all joy, knowing the rescuing of millions of souls—even just one—is worth it.

Our Attitude toward Suffering

Everyone, at some point or another, faces suffering, the soldier especially, because he has willingly put himself in a battle. However, it is not so much what we suffer, but *how* we suffer that matters. The way our heart responds to suffering is crucial, because by it we will either advance or become stagnant.

To suffer like a good soldier is to willingly endure all for the sake of the call. To suffer like a bad soldier is to grumble when difficult situations and hardship arise and to think, *Why me? Why all this suffering?* When we think or say things like this, we have forgotten we are soldiers and have forgotten the great cause for which we labor. Instead of throwing our lives into what God has called us to, we try to hold on to our lives, wanting to get away with as little suffering as possible, paying as little price as possible. We have forgotten that we are under orders and that we willingly gave up our lives.

Christ lived with the expectation of suffering. Throughout the Gospels, He repeatedly referred to the suffering that He would face. In Matthew 16:21, we are told that "Jesus began to explain to his disciples that he must go to Jerusalem and suffer many things at the hands of the elders, chief priests and teachers of the law, and that he must be killed." And again, in Mark 9:12, He said, "The Son of Man must suffer much and be rejected."

Jesus had the mind that with His call came suffering. But unlike many of us, He did not despise it. He willingly accepted it. In the Garden of Gethsemane the night He would be betrayed, Jesus cried out to God saying, "My Father, if it is possible, may this cup be taken from me. Yet not as I will, but as you will" (Matthew 26:39). Jesus had the mind and readiness to suffer if that was what the Father chose for Him.

We are told that our attitude toward suffering should be the same as Christ—"As Christ hath suffered for us in the flesh, *arm yourselves likewise with the same mind*" (1 Peter 4:1, KJV, emphasis mine).

Willingness to suffer is saying, "If I have nothing, that's okay. If I don't have a bed to sleep on, that's fine. If my leader asks me to serve through another two or three days after sleepless nights, that's fine. If I have to work all night at home, and the next morning still come to work, that's fine too."

Watchman Nee further explains this attitude toward suffering in his book, *The Character of God's Workman:*

> Having the mind to suffer speaks of my readiness before God to suffer. I am willing to go through trial . . . it is up to the Lord whether or not to put suffering in my path, but on my part I am always prepared to suffer. Thus when His providential change comes and trial falls upon me, I will not be surprised but rather feel that this is what I should go through in the first place.[1]

The issue is not necessarily outward circumstances. No, it goes much deeper, to the condition of our hearts. What is our attitude? When you have not slept for two nights and you are asked to go travel to the mission field, do you complain in your heart, saying, "I don't want to go. I need to get some sleep. This life is too hard"? If that be so, I pray you would repent before the Lord and ask Him to renew your love for and commitment to Him. For "to this you were called, because Christ suffered for you, leaving you an example, that you should follow in his steps" (1 Peter 2:21). Without this mind to suffer, you are not qualified to serve the Lord.

By His grace, I pray each of us would have this matter of suffering forever settled within our hearts, so that in the day of adversity we do not shrink back, but stand firm.

You see, without this mind to suffer, no one can last long in the kingdom of God. Why? Because "everyone who wants to live a godly life in Christ Jesus will be persecuted" (2 Timothy 3:12). When we don't have this mind in us, then the moment that suffering comes along, we can become angry and despondent and our work and love for the Lord cease. But if you have the mind to suffer, when faced with hardship and trial, lack of money, food, clothes, rejection, loneliness, pain and all kinds of assaults, you will not shrink back, because within you dwells a heart to suffer. Having the mind to suffer creates a sort of safeguard to the work the Lord has called us to, ensuring its progress.

An Awesome Weapon

It is a mistake to think of suffering as just a "necessary evil." It is not. The willingness to suffer is an awesome weapon. It is a sword, a pistol, a tank, even a hydrogen bomb to the enemy. It is a powerful instrument of war before which Satan is bound.

Do you grasp that? Satan is bound by the weapon called your willingness to suffer!

Throughout His ministry on earth, numerous times Satan tempted Jesus to avoid suffering and the cross. But in the end, the victory was won, and Satan was eternally defeated. How? Hebrews 2:14 tells us—"[Jesus destroyed] him who holds the power of death" through His *death on the cross*. It was not when Jesus healed the leper, raised the dead, fed the 5,000, walked on water or preached the Sermon on the Mount that He overcame Satan. No! Little did Satan know, laughing as Jesus was dying on the cross, that the Son of God would destroy him through that very death—through His suffering!

And this embracing of suffering is what we are called to imitate. Just like he did with Jesus, Satan tempts us to avoid suffering and the cross we are called to carry daily. Why? Because he knows that just as Christ defeated him through His suffering, we, too, defeat him and his forces when we are willing to follow in the footsteps of Christ and embrace suffering.

We must see the precious gift that suffering for the Gospel is. Remember that the times the Church was the strongest and most flourishing were the times it experienced great persecution. Even Paul confessed that the suffering he faced "really served to advance the gospel" (Philippians 1:12). When we have this kind of attitude, nothing becomes impossible.

We had four brothers in Orissa who were caught and beaten and their Bibles and books burned. As they were being dragged out of the village to be burned alive, a schoolteacher saw them and ran to the police station to report what was happening. Before the fanatics were able to kill them like missionary Staines and his sons, they were rescued from the incident by the police.

After the incident, these brothers wanted to go straight back to the place where they had just been beaten, desiring even more to see their persecutors come to Christ. They knew that they may be beaten again, and maybe even worse. But that was nothing if only they could preach the Gospel and see men turn to Christ.

What can the devil do to these kinds of people? Anything is possible for those who have this kind of readiness to endure whatever is necessary for the sake of reaching the goal. Oh, how I pray we would all have this kind of view toward suffering and, by it, see the Gospel go forth faster and stronger than ever before.

By Our Own Choosing

Someone else cannot impose a life of suffering and hardship on you. It is something individually you must choose. As Watchman Nee said, "In the Scriptures we find that to suffer is a path which we deliberately choose to take before the Lord."[2]

The Bible tells us we *choose* inconveniences, sleepless nights, difficulties, misunderstandings, the loss of our rights, the trashing of our reputations and the experience of being falsely accused. It is the path we choose!

In John 10:17–18, we see how Jesus made this choice, saying, "I lay down my life. . . . No one takes it from me, but I lay it down of my own accord." Over and over again, He continually made this choice to lay down His rights as the Son of God, ultimately consummating in His death. And even then, when the suffering of the cross came, when He was mercilessly beaten, spit on and mocked, instead of calling for legions of angels to come to His aid and stop it all, He *chose* to suffer.

We can say this is all good and necessary; we can know about the need to count the cost and accept suffering, but do we really choose this for our own lives?

If you want to do something significant with your life, you

simply must choose the path of suffering. It need not be suffering in the form of beatings, stonings, being knifed or having your Bibles burned. These things happen once in a lifetime and are not the suffering most of us will face. Rather, I am talking about daily living with the mind to let go of anything God asks us to release—sleep, a meal, a relationship, whatever. May our mind-set be, "Lord, how can I do one more thing, even if I don't like it, so the Gospel can be preached?" If you are not willing to live in this mind-set, then you are not fit to be among us.

Why do I say this to you? Because we are not playing games. Reaching the lost is not just a job or a good thing to do. I am convinced that with 1.5 billion people living on the Indian subcontinent and 40,000 of them going to hell every single day, our call is to spend our lives to see the Gospel preached. My call is not to be comfortable, to sleep all I want or even to enjoy my wife and kids. I must do everything I can to grab the multitudes that are dying before it is too late.

Do you want something other than this for your life? If so, please go serve somewhere else. I leave my wife and kids eight months of the year to travel like a madman, and I call you to be willing to do the same thing.

The servant of God should not be one who asks, "How can I find the most comfort? How can I have an easier life?" That is not the way of Christ. "For it has been granted to you on behalf of Christ not only to believe on him, but also to suffer for him" (Philippians 1:29).

Remember the words of Christ: "If anyone would come after me, he must deny himself and take up his cross and follow me" (Mark 8:34). You are called by God—not by me—to take up the cross with all its inconveniences, loneliness and extra work. No clock on the wall will tell you when you may stop working. No vacation from your responsibilities should be demanded. You have no grounds to make demands or claims on your own life because you chose to respond to the Lord's call to serve Him. Please don't forget that you are a soldier. You have no rights of your own.

Do you understand that? Without this understanding, the work of God would become just a business group or charity organization. We would not be servants of Christ without this readiness to pay the price and suffer all that is necessary to see the Gospel preached. We must be willing to choose this for ourselves and our families.

The work cannot wait for you. Whether or not you have food, nonetheless you must work. Whether you are clothed or not, you must nevertheless continue to serve the Lord. Whether you have comfort or distress, money or poverty, good report or bad report, good health or ill health, like a soldier you have one thing on your mind—the One who enlisted you and the purpose for which He called you.

Unmovable and Enduring

"Without a mind to suffer, you are subject to Satanic attack at this very point of your fear, and you will be finished. But if you declare, 'I am not afraid of sickness,' Satan will be bound."[3] Fear vanishes when you declare, "Satan, no matter what I face, I will not quit."

This willingness to suffer makes us unmovable and enduring. We must understand that this is the only way to reach the nations. We will never reach India, Bhutan, Myanmar, Nepal, Sri Lanka, Bangladesh or China with money. We won't reach these nations with big buildings or a popular name. We will only reach this generation with committed people who are willing to lay down their lives, who consider their lives nothing, their one goal being to finish the ministry the Lord gave them—to preach the Gospel. Only with men and women who look into the face of death and suffering and say, "Where is your sting?" will we reach these nations!

Amy Carmichael gave up all ambitions to be married and have a comfortable life in order to live and die as a missionary to India. She spent the greatest part of her life in pain, sick and bedridden, yet still she rescued hundreds of children from the hands of Satan. She started the Dohnavur Fellowship and is the one who scribbled these lines:

From prayer that asks that I may be
Sheltered from winds that beat on Thee,
From fearing when I should aspire,
From faltering when I should climb higher,
From silken self, O Captain, free
Thy soldier who would follow Thee.

From subtle love of softening things,
From easy choices, weakenings,
(Not thus are spirits fortified,
Not this way went the Crucified,)
From all that dims Thy Calvary,
O Lamb of God, deliver me.

Give me the love that leads the way,
The faith that nothing can dismay,
The hope no disappointments tire,
The passion that will burn like fire.
Let me not sink to be a clod:
Make me Thy fuel, Flame of God.[4]

None of us will do a single thing for the kingdom unless we have the mind to accept inconvenience. I am not urging you to give up your salary, sell your house, walk around naked or have no car or scooter. I am not telling you that because you are serving the Lord, you and your family must suffer in these ways. We don't do that, and I am not after people to make use of them, get the maximum out of them and then dump them on the roadside. Everyone has his own inconveniences. My inconveniences, suffering and difficulties are not yours. My difficulties may be your luxuries. I am telling you the reality that, as a soldier for Christ, you must be willing to pay whatever cost is required. We must continually choose the inconveniences that come in our lives for the sake of the kingdom. If we do not, we will not make it to the finish line. There's no way around it.

May the Lord give us the grace to embrace suffering just as Jesus did. I pray that you would open your heart and allow the Lord to show you the areas in which you may be looking for an easier road. I pray that we would repent before the Lord. Of all the words I know, the word *repent* is the most precious and means more to me than the words *grace* or *love*.

Why?

Because if you humble yourself and repent, saying, "Lord, my heart is cold. I am going after the things of the world. I am more concerned with my health and my comfort and my wife and kids than Your kingdom and Your people. Lord, I am more concerned about my comfort and future than the lost in the villages going to hell. Please forgive me, Lord. Would you change my heart?"—I tell you, something amazing will happen inside of you. His anointing, grace and peace will enter your life, drawing you closer and closer to His side and changing your heart to be one that is willing to give whatever He asks because of your love for Him.

Follow in the footsteps of Christ. Be one who is willing to suffer.

ten

principle-centered living

On September 24, 1988, at the Olympic Games held in Seoul, Korea, Canadian Ben Johnson ran the 100-meter dash in a remarkable 9.79 seconds, beating the old world record and making him the fastest human ever. He became the pride of his nation as he was awarded the gold medal for this triumphant act.

But the celebration came to a quick and devastating end when two days later Olympic officials entered the athlete's room and walked out with his gold medal—Ben Johnson had tested positive for the use of an illegal, performance-enhancing steroid.

In just a short time, this athlete's reputation and accomplishment turned sour. Why? Because he did not compete according to the rules.

You see, it did not matter how many years or how hard he worked to make it into the Olympics. It did not matter what country he ran for or how many people were cheering him on.

Nor did it make any difference what record he broke or how fast he ran. All of his accomplishments were worthless because he did not compete according to the rules marked out.

And so it is—if not more so—for us who are called into the ministry. As Paul said to Timothy, "If anyone competes as an athlete, he does not receive the victor's crown unless he competes according to the rules" (2 Timothy 2:5). In His Word, God has laid out the rules for the race we are running. It is especially crucial now, in a time when situational ethics and convenience have taken precedence, for us to go back to God's Word and search out His ways and instructions so that we can determine how to live according to His principles. It is our responsibility as servants of God to search out and study what God has to say about all the different aspects of our lives—family life, relationships, raising children, managing our time and money, controlling our tongue, responding to hurt, pain and misunderstanding, spiritual warfare, healing, the Holy Spirit, spiritual growth, caring for new believers, restoring those who are backslidden and many others. For through God's Word, He has "given us everything we need for life and godliness" (2 Peter 1:3).

Unchanging Principles

We should take notice of the fact that no athlete—to whom Paul compares the servant of God—makes up the rules of the game. They are preestablished by the authorities, with no gray areas. One must run strictly according to these rules or else he will lose, even if he is the first to cross the finish line.

In His Word, God has set particular rules and principles for how we must conduct ourselves in light of the calling with which He called us. These principles are fixed, firm and unbending. They are the lighthouse keeping us on the right course. No matter how huge or strong a ship may be, it must move based on the lighthouse's instruction. The lighthouse never moves. The ship must move. In the same way, the guidelines God gave us in His Word on how to live and serve Him are never going to change based on man's traditions or compromising. We are the ships, the ones that must steer our course in agreement with His unchanging principles. If not, we are in danger of running aground.

Because of this, we must stop often along the way as we serve God and ask ourselves, *Am I doing the work of God according to the instruction and guidelines He has given in His Word?* God is more concerned with how this race is run—in integrity and honesty before Him—than about how many churches are planted or how great the ministry looks. The end never justifies the means.

Consider if a mother were to try to get her child to go to sleep by saying, "Shhh! The devil is coming; you must fall asleep and not make any noise or he'll find you." The baby may close her eyes and stay quiet, and the mother may congratulate herself for the tactic working, but the way her child fell asleep was through fear and deceit. Who knows what far-reaching effects those lies and manipulation may have upon her daughter! The end may look all good and well, but the means was horribly wrong.

Our service for God must not follow this course of just getting the job done. We cannot be careless in how we live our lives or serve in the ministry. For the result of all that we do to be pleasing to the Lord, the means must be spiritual; otherwise, it will not last for eternity. Instead, it will be counted among the hay, wood and stubble Paul speaks about in 1 Corinthians 3:10–13, saying,

Each one should be careful how he builds. For no one can lay any foundation other than the one already laid, which is Jesus Christ. If any man builds on this foundation using gold, silver, costly stones, wood, hay or straw, his work will be shown for what it is, because the Day will bring it to light. It will be revealed with fire, and the fire will test the quality of each man's work.

May we be wise to take Paul's warning and be careful how we build. Many today are active in performing their ministries, but in the final analysis, all might be burned into a pile of ash because of the way it was accomplished. Before the world the ministry may seem impressive, yet when God looks upon it, He sees what it is really constructed of. If little or nothing was done in the power of the Holy Spirit or for the glory of God, it does not please Him and it will not last. We must run according to the rules He set out for us. No matter what we do, we must do it so that it will last on the day of judgment.

God have mercy upon us and help us to continue on the journey, seeking His face and following His principles, not only corporately but individually as well.

Principles to Live By

What are these principles God has given us, showing the way to serve Him effectively? What are the rules in this race He has called us to run?

I want to highlight 10 specific principles that I have made the priority in my life and service to God and that I believe will be helpful to you as you pursue the principle-centered life.

The first one that I have found crucial is *submission*. All of us are placed under some type of authority, and as Romans 13:1 tells us, "There is no authority except that which God has established."

Jesus demonstrated this principle in the way that He submitted His own life to the authority of His Father. He was not independent—a free individual running around doing whatever He wanted. Read through the Gospels and you will find Him repeatedly saying, "I do nothing of Myself" (see John 5:19, 30; 8:38; 12:49; 14:10). In the same way, we must be people of submission, willing to yield our rights and honor God by obeying the authorities He has set over us.

Another principle is *contentment*. Without a doubt, one of the main factors in believers becoming ineffective and falling away from the ministry is discontentment. Whether it be a love for money and material things, the seeking of praise and position or something else that pulls at us, we must be a people who are content with the life the Lord has chosen for us, able to say like David did in Psalm 16:5–6 (NKJV), "LORD, You are [my] portion. . . . The lines have fallen to me in pleasant places."

Contentment frees us from enslavement to men and circumstances when we are tempted with external stimuli toward the things of the world. Paul exhorts Timothy that "godliness with contentment is great gain" (1 Timothy 6:6).

The story of Gehazi in 2 Kings 5 is one illustration of a servant of God who was not content and as a result fell prey to the trap of the enemy. It was God's plan for Gehazi to be a prophet like his master, Elisha, and possibly even to receive a double portion of anointing, just as Elisha had. But Gehazi lost out and missed the opportunity. Why? Because although he knew the principle (and had the example of his master) that in serving God one should not seek money or personal benefit, when he was tested he failed; and in the end he became a leper.

So it was in the life of Balaam. He did not survive because he loved money and the things of this world more than he did God's principles. He was unwilling to obey God and keep the rules of the game and therefore was destroyed.

Forgiveness is another principle set for us to follow in this race. The reason it is so important is because there will never be a time when we are not hurt by someone's words or deeds. People will wrong us—even people who work with us in the ministry—and when they do, we must be quick to demonstrate Christ's love toward them through offering forgiveness. A servant unable to forgive from his heart comes under the judgment of God (see Mark 11:25). Oftentimes, God actually uses offenses to make us more like Christ. Refusing to forgive leads to bitterness, which will hurt us and, in the end, actually destroy our ministries. Therefore, the principle of forgiveness must become part of our daily lives.

Another principle we must live by is that of *faith*. Throughout our lives and ministries, we will face impossible situations. Putting unshakable confidence in the written Word of God and remaining steadfast in the faith developed through it anchor and enable us to see the impossible become possible. God says, "I am watching over my word to perform it" (Jeremiah 1:12, RSV). We must be people who "live by faith, not by sight" (2 Corinthians 5:7) if we want to run this race the right way.

Being absolutely *honest and truthful* is another principle we must not overlook as we continue this race the Lord has set us on. We must walk in the light before God and with one another (see 1 John 1:7). People often misrepresent facts for the sake of gaining approval. But to serve God in the right way, the way that pleases Him and brings Him honor, we must maintain honesty and truthfulness in our communication and dealings with people, no matter who they are.

Faithfulness is a most significant principle. No matter how educated, able or experienced a person is, he will never succeed without the virtue of loyalty in his heart and life. I know for myself that I would rather see a weak but faithful person handling responsibility and serving the Lord rather than a strong person who is not faithful. Faithfulness means that through thick or thin, good times or bad, we remain true to God and true to one another at all costs.

Humility is the foundation of God's grace and blessing in all we do, for He "opposes the proud but gives grace to the humble" (James 4:6). Pride will destroy our lives and ministries faster than anything else. Therefore, we must be careful how we run, making sure that it is in brokenness and humility, following Jesus, who was "humble in heart" (see Matthew 11:28–30).

The principle with which Christ summarized the whole of the Scripture is *love:* " 'Love the Lord your God with all your heart and with all your soul and with all your mind.' This is the first and greatest commandment. And the second is like it: 'Love your neighbor as yourself' " (Matthew 22:37–39).

In 1 Corinthians 13, Paul expounds upon this principle, saying that even if he had every gift and ability and accomplished great things but did not love, it would all be worthless. We must regard the principle of love as supreme in our lives and service, understanding the meaning of love and living it out in our words, attitudes, responses and actions. "By this all men will know that you are my disciples, if you *love* one another" (John 13:35, emphasis mine).

Another key principle as we run this race is that of *courage and boldness.* Our words and actions must be based on the truth of God's Word, which sinful man and this fallen world are often opposed to. Therefore, it takes courage and boldness on our part to stand up and live in the truth of His Word and follow Him. If we do so, following the principles of Scripture and being courageous to act on them regardless of the consequence or opposition, the ultimate victory will be ours. Sometimes we may have to stand alone and sometimes it may be costly, but it is worth it and pleases God. As we serve God, especially in the face of opposition from the enemy without and compromise from within, it takes courage to continue in the spiritual battle.

The last principle I want to mention is that of living a life of *unselfishness*. Our worst enemy in the ministry is often our own self-centeredness. How often we are tempted to grab for our own lives and look out for only ourselves! But as followers of Christ, we are called to lay down our lives for Him and for one another. In all areas, "it is more blessed to give than to receive" (Acts 20:35), and "the generous soul will be made rich" (Proverbs 11:25, NKJV).

Choose This Day

We would do well to order our lives according to these principles, choosing daily to align our lives with the truth of God's Word. You alone will be responsible for giving account for the manner in which you ran. Therefore, echoing Paul, I encourage you to run in such a way that you will win and need not be ashamed (see 1 Corinthians 9:24).

May the Lord strengthen you and give you the determination to stand before Him and fulfill the ministry to which He has called you and live by the unchanging principles of His Word. May we be careful how we build, taking the time to hear from Him, know His ways and imitate Him, refusing to follow the wisdom of this present world.

Living by godly principles carries a price. Are you willing to pay it?

eleven

a diligent servant

A day in the life of a farmer starts early and ends late. It's full of activity, most of which is physical labor—there are cows to milk, fields to plow, machinery to fix. The duties are endless and the day is tiring, but he continues to work day after day. Why? Because he knows that if he does, he will see the rewards in the harvest he reaps. That motivation keeps him going.

It is interesting then that Paul likens the servant of God to a farmer in 2 Timothy 2:6—"The hardworking farmer should be the first to receive a share of the crops." Paul wanted Timothy's perspective toward the ministry to be the same—one of seizing the time and working hard, with the harvest in mind. And notice how Paul didn't just say a farmer but a *hardworking* farmer. Why is this? Because not all farmers are hardworking!

Proverbs 24:30–34 speaks of one such farmer—a man who had a lot of land but whose fields were filled with thorns and weeds and whose walls were crumbling. The man was living in poverty. Why? Because he was not diligent to work. He was lazy and spent his time sleeping and doing nothing in particular.

Upon seeing this, the writer of the proverb says, "I applied my heart to what I observed and learned a lesson from what I saw: A little sleep, a little slumber, a little folding of the hands to rest—and poverty will come on you like a bandit and scarcity like an armed man" (Proverbs 24:32–34).

Notice that it wasn't a lot of slumber or a lot of rest—it was *little*. A farmer who continually works hard, on the other hand, reaps a bountiful harvest. As Proverbs 13:4 says, "The diligent are fully satisfied."

I am absolutely convinced that the personal life and effectiveness of a servant of God are directly proportionate to his commitment to work hard. I doubt seriously that God can use anyone not willing to commit himself to this kind of diligence.

Paul also understood this. He knew that no matter how much theology Timothy learned or how much understanding he had of Christian work and the needs around the world, nothing would make him effective unless he was willing to get up, set his hand to the plow and work hard, day after day being diligent in the service of the Lord.

This truth has not changed. There are many today who desire to do great things in the kingdom of God, many who have received ample training and have been placed in positions of great privilege where it would be easy to accomplish something significant, yet their lives produce no fruit! Why? Because they simply are lazy.

My brothers and sisters, this is a tragedy! In all things we are called to imitate Christ. Let us then get up and follow our Lord who, too, was hardworking. He was a man of diligence, faithfully laboring at the task the Father gave Him to do. Indeed, it was He who said, "My Father is always at his work to this very day, and I, too, am working" (John 5:17).

Growing up in a carpenter's home, Jesus certainly knew

what it meant to work hard. And when the Father told Him to begin His ministry on earth, He was quick to obey and work diligently. All throughout the Gospels, we find Him constantly on the move, preaching here, walking there, healing this person and praying for another. He never wasted a minute or opportunity, and He never took a vacation. Even when He sat down to rest from His journey, we find Him teaching His disciples and instructing them in the things of the kingdom. When He saw the multitudes—sheep without a shepherd—He was moved with compassion, and we find Him again doing ministry.

The men He called to be His disciples were also hardworking. In fact, I think one of the reasons He chose them was because He knew they would not be lazy. Fishermen were known to be some of the hardest workers of their day. They knew what it meant to diligently keep at a task until it was done, qualities that would be needed in the building of the kingdom of God.

Consider the time that Peter and John, after fishing all night without rest, were asked to make their boat available for Jesus to teach from (see Luke 5:1–7). They were certainly worn-out by the time morning came and probably were looking forward to a good meal and getting cleaned up. But they stayed on their boat and prepared it for the Lord to teach the multitudes. And after He was done, He told Peter and John to go back out fishing again! Imagine how you would feel after a hard night's work and a busy day of crowds and the Lord asking you to go back out to work hard. Yet they made no excuses. Rather, they obeyed and went the extra mile. That was hard work! And, as always, it paid off.

We, too, need to become people who are quick to follow our Master and diligently work at the task that He has given us, no matter what cost may come to our personal lives. Let us not make excuses and look for the easier, more relaxed road.

This life is short; we must do all that we can now, with this time we've been given, to bring many into the kingdom of God. Truly, the harvest is plentiful, but the laborers are few. May the Lord find many faithful, hardworking laborers among us whom He can send into His fields.

Taking Ownership

How does one become hardworking? Our flesh simply hates discipline and hard work, and by nature we tend to be lazy and like our rest. But in the work of the Lord, we simply cannot afford to. The souls of men and women are at stake. What is it, then, that moves us past our human tendencies and into this kind of committed life? The answer is *ownership*.

Have you ever read the history of Russia? When the Communists took over after the 1917 revolution, although Russia had been a major exporter of grain to the rest of the world, the nation then became so poor that its people had to stand in queue just to buy a single piece of bread.

What happened? The Communists set out to destroy capitalism and institute the ideas of socialism. This meant that all the farmers—the millions who owned a half acre, one acre, ten acres, a hundred acres or a thousand acres—had their land taken over by the government for them to divide the yield of the harvests "equally" among all people. Instead of the farmer working hard to produce enough food for his family and enough to sell for profit, each individual farmer was granted a fixed percentage of his own crop—all the rest now belonged to the government.

What was the result? Well, suppose I owned ten acres of land. I might say to my sons, "Why get up at three in the morning to begin our work? Whether we cut a thousand bushels of wheat today, a hundred, or just fifty, it makes no difference. We only get to keep so much anyway."

Their motivation died because their incentive had faded. As a result, production dramatically diminished until Russia, once among the top in wheat producers, had to import from other countries (a trend that the country today is still trying to reverse).

The same thing happens to us when we don't understand the principle of ownership. It was ownership that Paul wanted Timothy to grasp when he said, "Remember Jesus Christ, raised from the dead. . . . This is *my* gospel" (2 Timothy 2:8, emphasis mine). It did not belong to somebody else; Paul took ownership of the Gospel. It was not simply something he did to meet some requirement or to fill up his time. He took it as his *personal responsibility* to preach the Good News to those who had not heard.

We must have this same attitude in the work God has called us to. When you look at Rajasthan, Himachal Pradesh, Bhutan, Sikkim, China or Nepal and the millions of people who live in each of these regions, you must see them by faith and say, "They are *my* people, members of *my* church who belong to heaven and for whom Jesus died. I will not see them go to hell." When you feel that something is yours, when you begin to take ownership of the people living in your mission field, you begin to be consumed with prayer for them, your thoughts are constantly on them and faith builds up in you, spurring you on to do whatever it takes to get the job done and reach them despite all obstacles. You become like the hardworking farmer!

Well-Pleasing Servants

Are you a hardworking farmer, diligently plowing and harvesting in the fields God has appointed you to? By God's grace and mercy, I pray that each one of us would be able to say that this is true of ourselves, for this is the kind of servant with whom the Lord is well-pleased.

In Matthew 25, Jesus spoke about three men to whom He entrusted one with five talents, another with two, and the last man with one. The man with the five talents and the man with two took theirs, worked hard and increased the amount they had originally received. But the man who was given one talent did not work hard; he simply dug a hole in the ground and buried it. Of him Jesus said, "You wicked, lazy servant" (Matthew 25:26).

Those are serious words! They clearly show that God curses those who handle the Lord's work without diligence. It reminds me of an article I read some time ago that reported the average office worker in India who is paid eight hours' salary actually works fewer than two hours a day! As a result, production is almost nil. This kind of servant can be likened to a sloth. The sloth is the slowest-moving animal on earth, and it sleeps more than 15 hours a day. What a monkey could travel in a few minutes may take the sloth an entire day. Similarly, the servant of God who does not diligently work at the task his Master has given him may take a whole day to complete a job that the hard worker could finish in five hours.

I want to ask you, my brothers and sisters, have you set a target of how much you want to reap at harvesttime? Are you sowing those seeds so that when the time comes there will be a crop? Or do you have Gospel tracts sitting somewhere collecting dust? Do you sow seed wherever you go, looking for opportunities to minister to those around you in any way that you can? Do you have goals for spreading the Gospel?

My own brothers, you see, are farmers. All the time, their thoughts are toward their farms, continually thinking how they can get the most out of them. They may borrow money from the bank so that they can invest more into the harvest. They ask questions like, "Is this the right seed or the wrong seed? What we did last year didn't work. How can we get more crops out of this land?"

Are you like that about God's work? A plentiful harvest does not spring up from haphazard methods. You cannot just *imagine* 50 acres of rice or wheat and then go to sleep, praying, fasting and believing that when harvesttime comes, you will get the best yield in the whole world. Rather, you must work diligently, day after day, to plant and nurture in order to harvest a fine crop.

In Nepal and other places where it is difficult to grow produce and grains, farmers work extremely hard from early morning until late at night. Their time is given to prepare the ground, plow the fields, remove the rocks and cut down the thorns to ready the soil for planting. Everyone—wives, children, friends and hired people—works together to get all the work done. They chase the birds and monkeys away. They water, fertilize and watch diligently over the crop. Do you get a sense of the amount of organization and planning that goes into this?

In the same way, you must be diligent, sober and creative in the sowing, tending and reaping of your mission field's harvest. We must not be like the wicked, lazy servant whom God cursed. Instead, let us look for ways to increase what the Lord has entrusted us with, just like the man with five talents.

Long ago, one of our senior pastors in Northeast India began what he calls "salvation camp." These are events to which he calls all kinds of young people from Hindu, Muslim and Buddhist backgrounds together for several days. This brother and his team sing, preach and conduct many other activities during the camp. By the end, usually half of these young people give their lives to Christ. Not only that, but of those who are converted, he begins to think about which ones he can recruit to go and study in Bible college.

He came up with this idea because there were no Christian young people to recruit to be trained as missionaries. So he developed this plan to first bring people to Christ, as Paul did with Timothy, then recruit them to join him on the missionary journey. How marvelously God works in different ways in different places!

In your own mission field, you should be thinking of effective ways to reach the lost and work hard to do just that. Don't let anything stop you. Pray and ask the Lord for a plan and strategy for your mission field and then work hard toward that goal.

Think back to the type of person Timothy was. When Paul told him to be like the hardworking farmer, he was saying, "Timothy, I know the times are difficult. I know you are not strong physically and that you are sick to your stomach much of the time. But you won't be able to succeed unless you commit yourself to working as hard as a farmer. You must not be lazy. Redeem the time and give yourself fully to the work God has called you to."

Timothy had the call of God. Now he must apply himself to diligently work hard to fulfill that call, no matter what. If you lack fruit in your ministry and if God is not doing something significant through you, part of the problem may be that you are not a hardworking individual. May God give you the determination to not just hear from Him, but to work hard for Him as well.

Meditate on these verses about the success of the hard worker and the downfall of the lazy: Proverbs 6:6, 9; 10:26; 13:4; 15:19; 19:24; 20:4; 21:25; 22:13; 24:30–34; and 26:13–16.

Don't stop working; work harder than ever before and make this commitment: *Lord, I want to be efficient and do more than I am doing now in half the time!* My brothers and sisters, that is the way it should be. We are not merely working ordinary jobs. No matter what your task may be, realize that you have been called to be a part of establishing the kingdom of God upon this earth! It is a call worthy of your best time and effort, worthy of all that you are!

Let us then seize the opportunities and time God has given us and use them to reach the lost as soon as possible. This task is urgent and time is desperately short; yesterday—not just last year—is gone. We will never get that time back. Let us then give ourselves to our responsibility of reaching the lost world and saving the dying millions from hell.

The life of a servant of God who is deeply committed to the Lord and desperate to reach a lost world translates his commitment into hard work. May all of us in this movement be known as such people, living lives as focused and determined as the hardworking farmer, faithfully sowing and reaping, living with the harvest in mind.

There is no shortcut to success. Hard work is the key.

twelve

being a man of the Word

A servant of God is often known by how he handles the Word of God in his ministry. For that reason, one of the last things Paul told Timothy was, "Do your best to present yourself to God as one approved, a workman who does not need to be ashamed and who correctly handles the word of truth" (2 Timothy 2:15).

What does it mean to correctly handle the word of truth? It is not just a matter of understanding Scripture, but also applying it.

In James 1:22–25 we are told,

Do not merely listen to the word, and so deceive yourselves. Do what it says. Anyone who listens to the word but does not do what it says is like a man who looks at his face in a mirror and, after looking at himself, goes away and immediately forgets what he looks like. But the man who looks intently into the perfect law that gives freedom, and continues to do this, not forgetting what he has heard, but doing it—he will be blessed in what he does.

It is the man who lives in the Word of God and whose life is shaped and governed by it who is the kind of workman God approves.

This is especially crucial for today. We live in a generation with an incredible number of challenges to living a life according to the truth laid out in the Bible. On one hand there is pluralism and on the other hand liberalism. The uniqueness of Christ and the authority of Scripture are questioned on all sides. But regardless of the challenges made against it, the Word of God is the only true, sure and solid foundation for us to build our lives and ministry upon. Jesus assured us that "heaven and earth will pass away, but [His] words will never pass away" (Mark 13:31), "not the smallest letter, not the least stroke of a pen" (Matthew 5:18). God's Word "is eternal; it stands firm in the heavens" (Psalm 119:89). And God is "watching to see that [His] word is fulfilled" (Jeremiah 1:12).

In order for your life and ministry to be effective, you must be rooted in God's Word, for that alone is the only good seed, ensuring a good yield. If a farmer wants to reap a harvest of wheat, he doesn't plant corn seeds. He uses the right seeds— the wheat seeds. In just the same manner, you also must plant with the right seed—the Word of God—both in your personal life and in your ministry. No matter how hard you work or how many different things you try to do, it all means nothing if you don't have the right seed.

So, now knowing that the Word of God is the only good seed, infallible and sure to stand on, where do we begin in building our lives upon it? First things first—we must commit our time to studying His Word, finding out what it has to say to us individually as well as to the issues of life.

Committing Time to the Word

The image that the original Greek gives for "rightly dividing" is of someone able to cut a straight path through a thick forest. "In ancient times this word referred to the farmer who cut a straight furrow in the ground with his plow. Or woodcutters who would use their cutting tools to cut a straight path through the forest. Or stone masons who would use their tools to cut the stones straight so that they would fit in place. The whole idea is that one was familiar with one's tools and knew how to use them to get the desired results."[1] They skillfully used those tools to cut straight, *or rightly divide,* the word of truth.

If you were to look back throughout Paul's epistles, you would find how numerous times he had to bring correction to the different churches, setting straight where they had begun to divert from the truth of Scripture and bringing them back into alignment with what it has to say. He knew how to use his tool—God's Word—to bring about the desired result. From this, we catch a glimpse into the importance Paul placed upon God's Word and the weight with which he now called Timothy to do the same.

But, as is obvious, Paul didn't learn the truths of the Scripture overnight. It took time. In order for Timothy to follow Paul in properly handling God's Word, he, too, must simply commit his time to studying the Scriptures. Just the same, we, too, must also make the same commitment—cultivating a daily, disciplined approach to spending several hours in the Word of God, studying and meditating and asking the Holy Spirit to teach us its truths. We cannot be effective in the kingdom of God without this.

But this is not necessarily an easy, convenient element to implement into our lives. We are busy men and women, and life only seems to get busier. That is why we must make this a *commitment*. Defined, the word *commitment* means "the trait of sincere and steadfast fixity of purpose . . . the act of binding yourself to a course of action."[2] It implies going beyond convenience to the action of making time for what is most necessary and important to us.

Committing time to the study of God's Word means that whatever our days are filled with or how busy our lives become, we make the time to sit quietly before the Lord and allow Him to search our hearts and teach us from His Word. We do this because we understand and believe that it is from this foundation alone that good fruit comes to our lives and ministries.

I remember awhile ago, one of our senior leaders, a godly man whom I love dearly, said to me, "I don't know how to tell you this, but I feel a little dry and very discouraged. My heart cries out to know Jesus more, but I just don't have the time. I am running here and there in my travels and feel I don't have the time anymore to know Him."

"Brother," I replied, "I know what that is like. I understand. My life is also very busy. May I share with you how I've learned to dwell in the Word even so?"

He openly listened as I shared with him how, very long ago, I made the commitment that no matter what, I would make time to be in the Word daily. Even now, no matter how busy my life gets, every day I seek to get up at least an hour and a half to two hours early and study my Bible in the quietness of the early morning. I am absolutely sure that if I didn't do that, I would backslide more severely than anyone I know.

I am not telling you these things to promote myself but to illustrate the importance of being steadfast in the Word. In the years that I've been in the ministry, I have known countless people who have made a shipwreck of their lives simply because of this one fact: They were not spending time in God's Word. Lack of being in the truth of the Bible is the root of all our problems, because without the Word of God, no life-bringing transformation can take place within us. "For the word of God is living and active. Sharper than any double-edged sword, it penetrates even to dividing soul and spirit, joints and marrow; it judges the thoughts and attitudes of the heart" (Hebrews 4:12).

If we are not spending time in the Word of God and allowing it to judge and correct the thoughts and attitudes of our hearts, then the thorns and briars of sin will surely overtake us. But if we remain in Him who is the Word (see John 1:1), then we will continue to grow and bear good fruit, just as Jesus said in John 15:7—"If you remain in me and my words remain in you, ask whatever you wish, and it will be given you."

Do you spend at least an hour or two every single day reading, studying and meditating on God's Word? Or do you feel too busy to study God's Word? I assure you, God has not given you more than you can handle. In light of that, it is of utmost importance that you make the commitment to spend time in His Word. If you are a pastor of a congregation of any kind, ten members or ten thousand, you must spend at least two to three hours several days a week studying and preparing to teach the people in your congregation.

We must purpose to daily meditate on it throughout the different tasks of the day and to use every opportunity given to us—time in the morning, while we're waiting in queue, in our conversations and before we go to bed—to stay in the Word, following the commandment given to the children of Israel to "not let [the Word] depart from your mouth; meditate on it day and night, so that you may be careful to do everything written in it. Then you will be prosperous and successful" (Joshua 1:8).

My brothers and sisters, may I encourage you to make a fresh commitment today to read and study the Word of God like no other book? Doing any form of ministry without spending time in God's Word is inconceivable—empty and useless. May the Lord create in us a fresh and renewed hunger to this end.

Internalizing the Word

The truth of the commitment we must make to stay in the Word of God will never change. We must always give of our time and energy to study it and know what it says about the different aspects of life, learning how to live by it.

But in this we must be warned, carefully seeing to it that we do not fool ourselves by being only hearers of the Word and not doers, as James 1:22 warns us. There are many Bible students today studying all different facets of theology, but many are deceiving themselves because they are not acting upon the Word. You can study the Word of God for four hours every morning, but if you are not allowing the Spirit of God to use the Word to change and shape your heart, all study is useless.

Some Christian circles emphasize the importance of the Spirit of God. Others place the emphasis on the Word of God. But it is both working together in our lives that cause good fruit to bear. You see, the Spirit of God must never be separated from the Word of God. Together they must be able to do their good work within us. If this does not happen, if they are separated, we can have a lot of head knowledge about the Bible, but our lives will bear no witness to its transforming power. And those whose lives do not match what they preach are unfit to minister God's Word. If they have squabbles and disunity in their homes while trying to preach on love and unity and grace and forgiveness, their message is diluted by their duplicity. This is the kind of workman God does not approve of.

I remember an encounter I had with God in my early years of studying at seminary and pastoring a church in the United

States. My father-in-law came to visit from Germany, and we took him all around the town we lived in, as well as the school I was studying at. When he met some of my professors, many of them told him, "Your son-in-law is one of the brightest students we have ever had here." My father-in-law was quite happy to hear that, and so was I. Night after night I studied hard, searching through different commentaries and acquiring as much knowledge about the Scriptures as I possibly could. I became so dogmatic about my doctrines, so confident in my theological views that I even looked for opportunities to argue, debate and prove points to other people. I knew I had studied hard and knew a lot about the Scriptures, and those comments only reinforced my confidence.

But one afternoon the Lord spoke to me, knowing how proud my heart had become. He said to me, "You study the Bible so you can be smart and preach to your people. You stay up all night studying so you can be a good Bible teacher. You spend time with the Bible, but not with Me!"

You see, the truth of the Word of God was not penetrating my heart and transforming my own life. Each Sunday as I went before the people God called me to pastor, I was not handling the Word of God properly—I was spending a lot of time studying it and memorizing it, but was not allowing the Holy Spirit to use it to reveal my own heart and change my own life. I was merely full of knowledge, a carnal Christian, self-centered, arrogant and prideful. Because all the things I knew were never internalized, they were useless in the sight of God. I am so grateful that in His grace He came to me and corrected me, helping me to be the kind of worker He does approve of.

God did not give us the Bible to make us smart or so we could argue about it. He gave us His Word to change our lives. When that happens—when it becomes part of our lives—then we are handling it correctly when we preach. When I understood this, my life was transformed, and I was enabled to do what I am doing today.

You see, the Word of God is our contact with God the Father and His contact with us. As we study and live in it, it becomes a mirror for us to see the face of the Lord Jesus Christ (see 2 Corinthians 3:18). The Holy Spirit works inside us, taking the words, images, examples, commandments, exhortations, admonitions and warnings in God's Word and by it transforming us into the image of Christ. This is why Scripture tells us, "Let the word of Christ dwell in you richly as you teach and admonish one another" (Colossians 3:16). By it we gain the wisdom needed to carry out the ministry given to us by the Lord Jesus.

Jesus said, "As the Father has sent me, I am sending you" (John 20:21). As we go forth in the name of the Lord Jesus Christ, proclaiming His Word to the world, it is important that we become like Jesus so we can do the ministry of Jesus. The Word of God is the medium the Holy Spirit uses to convert us from the inside out and to make us like Jesus.

When we follow this path—committing time to the Word and allowing it to change our lives—we can be sure that the good seed of God's Word will produce a good crop within us.

May God give each of us the grace to be doers of the Word so that we may then be faithful proclaimers and rightfully handle the word of truth.

The Gospel Alone

The call of a pastor and teacher is revealed in John 21:17, when Jesus told Peter to "feed my sheep." What, then, do we feed the people of God with? Only with the unchangeable, life-giving truth—the Word of God.

Unfortunately, one of the greatest tragedies in Christendom

today is the increasing number of pastors and teachers who feed the people of God with the latest psychology, philosophy, stories and whatever else they can use to keep their ratings high and keep their jobs as pastors. Instead of being the only truth to live by and pure milk to help others grow and mature in faith, the Bible has become a tool of the trade. Instead of seeking to build up the people of God on the solid foundation of biblical truth, churches seek new ways to draw people in and entertain them. Sadly, these pastors are falling away from their true purpose—to study the Word, live in it and proclaim it without adulterating it with man's ideas and traditions.

In Romans 1:16, Paul said, "I am not ashamed of the gospel, because it is the power of God for the salvation of everyone who believes." If the Gospel alone has the power to save, it is the Gospel alone we should be preaching, being careful not to give in to tradition, new ideas or our own agendas as we seek to proclaim the message of God. Remember, God's thoughts and ways are what we must declare, and as Isaiah 55:8–9 tells us, "My thoughts are not your thoughts, neither are your ways my ways, declares the LORD. As the heavens are higher than the earth, so are my ways higher than your ways and my thoughts than your thoughts." Where are His thoughts and ways revealed to us? In Scripture.

The Bible then is the only true foundation on which we can build our message. A servant of God, whether a missionary on the field or a pastor with a congregation, is called by the living God to proclaim God's Word to sinners and saints—to sinners so they may hear the message of salvation, repent and be saved and to saints so that they may hear the Word of God, grow, mature in faith and be conformed to the image of Christ. The Bible is the complete and infallible revelation of the living God to mankind. It is indispensable for true evangelism and the making of disciples. Without the Word of God, we have nothing worth listening to, nothing to say and no hope of any success. But if we base our message or teaching on the Bible, it will bring forth the results God intends, just as Isaiah 55:10–11 says,

> As the rain and the snow come down from heaven, and do not return to it without watering the earth and making it bud and flourish, so that it yields seed for the sower and bread for the eater, so is my word that goes out from my mouth: It will not return to me empty, but will accomplish what I desire and achieve the purpose for which I sent it.

I believe the best, most thorough way to accomplish this is by the Inductive Bible Study method—teaching the whole counsel of God by going verse by verse from Genesis to Revelation—which all of our pastors are required to master. By doing this, people get the full content of God's revelation and thereby grow in their faith. Some of the most stable and growing churches in our generation are those in which the Word of God is taught in this way, with application made, so that people's lives are transformed.

Fruit of the Word

By studying the Word of God, our minds are renewed and our faith is built, for "faith cometh by hearing, and hearing by the word of God" (Romans 10:17, KJV). For us to accomplish the work of God and see His kingdom established, we must have faith, for without faith it is impossible to please God (see Hebrews 11:6).

My brothers and sisters, we are called to a great task, far beyond what mere man could ever hope to accomplish in and of himself—the task of proclaiming the Good News of salvation for sinners. But it is only through faith that sinners are saved. It is through faith that the sick are healed and demons are cast out. Impossible things are accomplished only through faith. And faith only comes by the Word of God! Hebrews 11 talks about those who through faith conquered obstacles and established God's kingdom in their generation. Where do we get this faith to move mountains and drive out the hosts of demons and hell and see millions come to know the Lord? Again, only from the Word of God! We must be people who live in and by the Word of God so that we may have the faith to see our generation won for Christ.

When we dwell in the Word of God, not only does our faith grow stronger, but we walk in its authority and power. As Paul said in 1 Thessalonians 1:5, "Our gospel came to you not simply with words, but also with power, with the Holy Spirit and with deep conviction." No Christian worker can be effective without authority and power, and no one can have authority and power apart from God's Word.

You can see the absolute importance, then, of studying and living constantly in the Word of God!

We must keep the Word before us day and night, meditating on it, living it and never letting it depart from our sight. Like a sponge, may we be saturated, filled and then overflowing with the Word of God, being the kind of worker of whom God approves. I pray this may be true of each one of us as we continue in the ministry. By God's grace, I believe it can be so.

Know the Word. Live the Word.

thirteen

set apart to walk
in holiness

Ministry is not just something one does.

Rather, it is the very extension and overflow of the inner life. For this reason, our inner life must be made pure and kept holy so that we can continue to be used for the purposes of God. Paul illustrated this truth in 2 Timothy 2:20–21, when he told Timothy,

> In a large house there are articles not only of gold and silver, but also of wood and clay; some are for noble purposes and some for ignoble. If a man cleanses himself from the latter, he will be an instrument for noble purposes, made holy, useful to the Master and prepared to do any good work.

The picture that Paul painted was very clear and still holds relevance today. Every house has utensils of different kinds used for different purposes. Through this passage, we see this is the same way it works in the kingdom of God, some vessels being used for noble purposes and some ignoble—all based upon whether or not the vessel is cleansed.

The reason Paul says these things to Timothy is because he knows that if Timothy does not continue to keep himself clean and holy, he cannot be used for noble purposes. Yet Paul's reasons go deeper still, far beyond just mere actions and doing all the right things on the outside—studying the Word, preaching the Word and obeying the Word. Paul is deeply concerned that Timothy's *heart* be pure and holy, truly set apart for the Lord. Why? Because it is out of our hearts that our ministry flows. As Jesus said in Luke 6:45, "For out of the overflow of [the] heart [the] mouth speaks." And "every good tree bears good fruit, but a bad tree bears bad fruit" (Matthew 7:17). If Timothy's inner life corresponds with all that he says and does, he will continue to bear good fruit.

Holiness Within

As Paul was stressing to Timothy the importance of a pure and holy heart, there were many of the opposite in their day. The Pharisees were a religious people totally concerned with the outward opinions of holiness, yet on the inside they were evil and rotten. Jesus spoke some of the harshest words against these pretenders (see Matthew 23).

Our times are not so different. A person can do all the right things and their ministry look to be so effective and godly, but it very well may not be the case. So many Christian workers are just playing the role, pretending to be godly to make a good impression on others. Because of this, their lives stay in deception and they travel further and further down this deadly road, becoming more and more evil as they have to keep on pretending to keep up the image. Not until the weight of hypocrisy is removed by their own choice to be cleansed by God can they then be made holy and pure from within.

We must be on guard and wise in today's world of Christianity. This means that we must not just assume that because one's ministry looks to be successful that the person's life is holy and he is a good example to follow. There is a serious misunderstanding that if a man has tremendous gifting and does great things for God, he must be God's favorite or a special, holy individual. Throughout the Old Testament, there are several places where God uses heathen kings to fulfill His plan (see Jeremiah 25:9; 27:6; 43:10; Isaiah 44:28; 45:1). And in Matthew 25, we read about a bunch of people who drove out many demons and performed great and mighty miracles all in the name of Christ. But on the day of judgment their true hearts are revealed, and God's response to them was that He never knew them. "Many will say to me on that day, 'Lord, Lord, did we not prophesy in your name, and in your name drive out demons and perform many miracles?' Then I will tell them plainly, 'I never knew you. Away from me, you evildoers'" (Matthew 7:22–23).

In 2 Kings 4:8–9, we see that the prophet Elisha was known for his holiness rather than for any spectacular thing he had done. There was no mistaking he was a man set apart for the Lord from within his heart. As Elisha walked among his contemporaries and spoke on behalf of a holy God, those who watched him knew he was a holy man. They may have forgotten his messages, but they could not forget the impact his life made on them.

This is not a phony, superficial impression that we try to make on others by using the right words and fluctuating our voices and our prayers or preaching. Rather, it is a quiet, deep life that comes from separation from self, the world and the work of darkness to instead pursue intimacy with the Lord.

May our prayer be that of David in Psalm 139:23–24 (NLT), "Search me, O God, and know my heart; test me and know my thoughts. Point out anything in me that offends you, and lead me along the path of everlasting life."

How We Are Made Holy

Notice the way Paul explains this principle of being cleansed and made holy in 2 Timothy 2:21—*"If a man . . ."* Scripture makes it clear that some kind of choice for self-purification on our part is absolutely necessary if one wants to be useful to Christ and His kingdom. It is the responsibility of the individual to take God seriously and make those choices (which may involve a lot of suffering) so that he can be that kind of individual God can use.

Brother or sister, let me ask you: What kind of choices are you making? Are they the ones that will lead you to be the kind of pure and holy vessel that God can use for noble purposes? I urge you to ask the Lord to evaluate your life.

Consider this: If someone brings you food on a plate, would you eat off the same plate next time without washing it first? Or would somebody else take your plate and eat from it? No, the plate would be washed first so it would be clean for future use. And so let us open our hearts to the Lord's searching that we might be continually cleansed and made "useful to the Master, prepared to do any good work." For God calls each one of us to "be ye holy; for I am holy" (1 Peter 1:16, KJV).

But how can we be holy?

Simply put, to be holy is to be like Jesus, who lived His life on this earth to do the will of His Father. "The essence of all sin is found in doing one's own will. And the essence of holiness in a human being is found in denying one's own will and in doing the will of God,"[1] just like Jesus did. Over and over again throughout the Gospels, Jesus said, "I do not seek My own will, but the will of Him who sent Me. . . . I have come not to do My own will. . . . Not as I will, but as You will" (see John 5:30; 6:38; Matthew 26:39, NKJV). When we yield our will, the Holy Spirit is then free to work in our lives and make us like Christ. As we make the choices toward this direction, laying down our selfish desires for the purposes of God just like Jesus did, we begin to be holy as He is holy.

So then, to live a life of continuous holiness and purity from within is only possible as we look to Jesus and seek His will above our own. There are many different areas the Lord may see we need to be cleansed of, and some of those require a continual cleansing. I want to highlight four specific areas I have found we can easily be defiled by and that the Word of God warns us about.

Specific Areas to Guard

One of the major areas that we need to continually be cleansed of and guard ourselves from is what we say and hear. This is very serious. A servant of God destroys himself sooner than he realizes by listening to and sharing in evil talk or gossip. Because of the potency of this poison, Paul tells Timothy to "shun profane and idle babblings, for they will increase to more ungodliness" (2 Timothy 2:16, NKJV).

In his book *Needed: Men of God*, Zac Poonen quotes Watchman Nee on this matter, who said, "If a Christian worker talks unadvisedly about all sorts of things, how can he expect to be used of the Lord in the utterance of his words? If God has ever put His word on our lips, then a solemn obligation is upon us to guard these lips for His service alone. We cannot offer a member of our bodies for His use one day, and the next day take it back for the use at our own discretion. Whatever is once presented to Him is eternally His."[2]

The second area we must continually cleanse ourselves from is that of bitterness and unforgiveness. One of the saddest things is the turmoil people live with because of not forgiving and letting go of hurts. This destroys people more than anything else.

Paul, and Timothy as well, had plenty of disappointments and people who had deserted them and violated their rights. It is the same with many of us. People will always fail us and hurt us. God is aware of this truth yet still tells us to quickly forgive those who wrong us: "Do not let the sun go down while you are still angry, and do not give the devil a foothold" (Ephesians 4:26–27).

The way we respond to hurt and disappointment is crucial. By keeping ourselves free from any root of bitterness, we ensure that the enemy will not have a foothold in our lives. Then we can continue to be used by God to show His love and goodness to those around us.

The third area is that of pride within our hearts. This is nothing but extreme self-centeredness and unbrokenness within. The hardness of heart that pride creates has been the downfall of many servants of God. It's the greatest deception of the enemy and the very thing that cast him from his place in heaven. When our hearts become contaminated with pride, God resists us. But as we stay humble before God and man, our lives are covered with His grace (see Proverbs 3:34).

A fourth area from which we must cleanse ourselves is the grip of materialism, for "no one can serve two masters. Either he will hate the one and love the other, or he will be devoted to the one and despise the other. You cannot serve both God and Money" (Matthew 6:24). Many precious men of God have been destroyed because of a love of money that slowly crept into their hearts.

No one, not even Timothy, is above this deception and these tools the enemy uses to tear us down. Each of us must be careful to guard our hearts and continually cleanse ourselves of all these things that pollute our ministry and effectiveness for God. We who began well must continue well. We do this by a constant cleansing.

Don't Be Fooled

During wintertime in the northern Arctic regions, everything is normally covered by ice, and the temperature easily reaches -60° C. The Eskimos who live in this frigid region survive by ice fishing or by hunting wolves. For centuries, they have had a unique way of hunting wolves. "First the Eskimo coats his knife blade with animal blood and allows it to freeze. Then he adds another layer of blood, and another, until the blade is completely concealed by frozen blood.

"Next, the hunter fixes his knife in the ground with the blade up. When a wolf follows his sensitive nose to the source of the scent and discovers the bait, he licks it, tasting the fresh frozen blood. He begins to lick faster, more and more vigorously, lapping the blade until the keen edge is bare. Feverishly now, harder and harder, the wolf licks the blade in the Arctic night. So great becomes the craving for blood that the wolf does not notice the razor sharp sting of the naked blade on his own tongue nor does he recognize the instant at which his insatiable thirst is being satisfied by his own warm blood. His carnivorous appetite just craves more—until the dawn finds him dead in the snow!"[3]

Why do I tell this story? Because it is an example of what can happen to us too. The animal did not know that his thirst for more blood would cause his own life to be cut into pieces.

Nor do we realize the self-destruction of just a little sin.

Please be aware. We should not be blind to think that things will work out automatically if we are not careful to keep our hearts pure. The enemy will not deceive us in one big, major event. No, it will be gradual, a slow creeping deception, happening so subtly that we, like the wolf, don't even realize what is happening until we are on the brink of destruction. But by protecting our hearts and minds from the devices of the enemy, we are kept in the safety of God.

In following the Lord there must be a continually renewed commitment to set ourselves apart to be pure vessels, ready for the Holy Spirit to use for God's glory. May we fulfill the call to personal holiness by heeding the Scripture and cleansing ourselves from the things that defile our hearts and ministry.

Be set apart for holiness.

fourteen

grace for failure

The kingdom of God is filled with people of all kinds. There are those who cannot walk well, some who are half-blind, some who are strong and good-looking and some who are not. Yet we all have this the same: No one can honestly say that he always does everything right (see 1 John 1:8).

It is inevitable, then, that in the kingdom of God we will fail and people will fail us. God did not choose us and call us into service because we were perfect individuals. We are learning and growing and, at times, failing.

Paul's understanding and experience of this truth are what compelled him to share with Timothy how to respond to the one who fails, saying, "The Lord's servant must not quarrel; instead, he must be kind to everyone, able to teach, not resentful" (2 Timothy 2:24).

The issue Paul was addressing was not so much whether a person fails or not. That will most certainly happen. What is important is our *response* to these failings.

Even when Jesus called the 12 disciples, He anticipated, by virtue of their humanity, that they would fail at times. And when they did, even with the one who betrayed Him, His response was always one of grace and love. I am sure that Jesus knew all along that Judas had been stealing money. Had I been Jesus, I would have kicked him out immediately. But, thank God, Jesus is not like that! Even the night before He was crucified, Jesus never disclosed the identity of His betrayer. Rather, He protected his dignity and said nothing evil about him. Jesus loved all the disciples until the very end.

Even when David, the great psalmist, turned into an adulterer and murderer, God still called him "a man after his own heart" (1 Samuel 13:14). God did not excuse his failing, but He responded with grace—and we must do the same.

The Failings of Paul and John Mark

If we read through Acts and consider what Paul's life was like, we can hear the words he spoke to Timothy ring with personal experience.

Remember John Mark, the young man spoken of in the book of Acts who accompanied Paul on one of his missionary journeys (see Acts 12:25)? I think that when Paul wrote to Timothy about how to handle failure, he was confessing his own weakness in his attitude toward John Mark. You see, this young brother had traveled on Paul's Gospel team but soon grew discouraged and turned back halfway through the journey. When John Mark later wanted to rejoin the team and serve God, Paul refused.

Barnabas, Paul's teammate and the one who first welcomed and befriended Paul as a new convert, tried to reason with him concerning John Mark. "Please understand that this young fellow is still learning," he said. "Yes, he failed, but let's take him anyway. He'll be better."

I don't know if this is the conversation that really took

place, but Acts 15:39 says, "They had such a sharp disagreement that they parted company." This was an outright quarrel. Paul was a militant, aggressive, disciplined and absolutely black-and-white leader who said, I imagine, "No way. He's no good. I don't want anybody like him on my team. I will not take this young man back because he did not keep his commitment. He failed. No second chance for him."

Barnabas, on the other hand, was a kind man who probably responded saying, "Paul, you so quickly forget where you came from! Don't you remember what a wicked man you were? Have you forgotten your own failings? Yet God had mercy on you. Nobody believed you or trusted you, but I opened my door to you. When people wanted to throw stones at you, I stood in front of you to protect you. I can't believe you won't show kindness to this young man who made a mistake."

But Paul continued to refuse. "No way, Barnabas. I meant what I said. I won't change." And so these two intimate friends, Barnabas and Paul, departed their separate ways—Paul with Silas, and Barnabas with John Mark.

But here, as Paul is saying his last words to Timothy, he adds this request: "Get Mark and bring him with you, because he is helpful to me in my ministry" (2 Timothy 4:11). This is the same John Mark that Paul earlier booted out, even though Barnabas tried his best to keep the young man on the team.

Why is Paul now asking for John Mark? What has happened since they parted ways? John Mark, the one who lost heart, the one Paul thought would not make it, had changed . . . and so had Paul.

The one who was once rigid, demanding and unwilling to offer grace to the one who had failed, had changed. He became a person of grace. And the one who had failed, because there was someone to come alongside of him to restore and help his walk, became useful for the ministry and wrote the Gospel of Mark.

It was Paul's own failure to show grace that was probably the reason for him emphasizing to Timothy the importance of having a loving attitude toward those who fail. It took Paul a long time to learn this lesson, and he wanted Timothy to understand this principle from the beginning.

Remember this story when similar circumstances come to you. Not every believer is completely mature. Hearts may be good and the desire to serve genuine, but that does not mean they will not fail. This does not mean to condone sin, but don't be one who goes around trying to expose people and their failures. Always ask, "If God did that to me through somebody else, how would I face it?" Be gracious, gentle and loving when dealing with people who have failed.

My brothers and sisters, you will have people who fail in the ministry and do some really stupid things. But if somebody fails, no matter what that person has done, we can forgive him. Whatever sin he has committed—even stealing money or falling into adultery—if he repents, please restore him. Don't let anyone on earth know about it. Love him, disciple him and strengthen him. Don't ever hurt a brother or sister if he or she repents.

The Fallen Peter

It was over. The one who not very long ago boasted that he'd follow Jesus wherever He went, even to death, had failed. Not just once, but three times he had openly denied ever even being with the man from Galilee. He who had given up his fishing boat to follow the anticipated king of Israel, was now left with nothing but the sting and heartache of his epic failure.

I wonder what had been going through Peter's mind as he went back to his fishing boat in John 21. He was returning to his old life, thinking maybe there was nothing left to do now.

Perhaps all that his Master spoke of ran through his mind, his own memories mocking him because of his failure. Peter probably had given up on himself. And now, even as he returned to his old life, he couldn't even do that well, not catching a single fish all night long.

But as morning came, so did Peter's restoration—through grace. Jesus was standing on the shore, and after telling him and John where to catch more fish than their nets could hold, He made breakfast for them by the sea.

Can you imagine how Peter might have felt, this being the first time with the risen Lord, knowing that Jesus knew he had forsaken and denied Him in His time of great distress? But every questioning thought of his was met with the purest grace and love from the very One who would be justified in His rebuke of him.

> When they had finished eating, Jesus said to Simon Peter, "Simon son of John, do you truly love me more than these?"
> "Yes, Lord," he said, "you know that I love you."
> Jesus said, "Feed my lambs."
> Again Jesus said, "Simon son of John, do you truly love me?"
> He answered, "Yes, Lord, you know that I love you."
> Jesus said, "Take care of my sheep."
> The third time he said to him, "Simon son of John, do you love me?"
> Peter was hurt because Jesus asked him the third time, "Do you love me?" He said, "Lord, you know all things; you know that I love you."
> Jesus said, "Feed my sheep" (John 21:15–17).

This is the most beautiful picture of grace for failure that ever has been. The Son of God, the epitome of perfection, just and perfect in all His ways, offering grace and restoring the very one who had failed Him. Three times He reinstated Peter, one for every denial. And not only that, but He placed responsibility of the ministry in his hands. Peter had failed; but grace still had a place for him.

Later in his life, Peter, remembering his own weakness and, greater still, the strength of the Lord's abundant grace to him, wrote these words: "The God of all grace, who called you to his eternal glory in Christ . . . will himself restore you and make you strong, firm and steadfast" (1 Peter 5:10).

Think about those words and the personal experience they came from! Peter had known firsthand the God of all grace, who Himself had restored him and out of his failure made him strong, firm and steadfast.

Please, let us be the very same as our Savior in this manner. If He who knew no sin could offer this kind of grace, how much more should we, sinners alike, extend grace to one another.

Generous with Grace

Not one of us is above any failure and able to discount and write off the servant of God who has failed in the smallest or greatest way. We must remember this especially when we are in the seat of advantage—the lender dealing with the one whose debts have not been paid, the parent dealing with the child, the leader with the young workers, the pastor with his congregation.

The heart of this message is especially for you who are strong to not forget where you have come from or the ways you have failed. Remember the grace that has been offered to you, no matter how small or great in measure, and return it to the younger and weaker one.

Maybe you have failed in life and have done something

really bad. Maybe you are living with fear because of the ways you have failed. I, too, have many failures and problems in my own life. There are times when I speak harsh, strong words, and afterward I feel sad about my statements. There is nothing to justify such harsh statements. I know my own failings. It is because of this that I strive to be a leader who continually offers grace, desiring that if I err, to err not on the side of justice but of grace.

Here is my heart: I would rather have a bunch of failing, wounded soldiers who are humble and broken and who want to serve God than a group of men who think they are perfect and who say, "I have never failed!" It is hard to live with such people. I am not promoting failure or sin. But if you have failed at anything in life, I want you to know that in repentance are grace and restoration. I do not ask that you are perfect, but only that you are honest in your heart and testimony before God.

Hear what Paul was saying to Timothy: Timothy, there will be many struggles along the way, but let your attitude not be one of bitterness. Be gentle and kind with those who fail, knowing the grace that you yourself have received.

Will you be like your Master? Will you be full of grace?

fifteen

man of discernment

What does it mean to be a man of discernment, and why is it important? Defined, *discernment* means "the keenness and accuracy of mental vision . . . the power of seeing deeply into a subject in spite of everything that intercepts the view."[1] A discerning man is not easily misled; a person with a penetrating mind sees a multitude of things that escape others, and his judgment detects the slightest differences.

The importance for the servant of God to be discerning is revealed in 2 Timothy 3:1–5, where Paul writes,

> But mark this: There will be terrible times in the last days. People will be lovers of themselves, lovers of money, boastful, proud, abusive, disobedient to their parents, ungrateful, unholy, without love, unforgiving, slanderous, without self-control, brutal, not lovers of the good, treacherous, rash, conceited, lovers of pleasure rather than lovers of God—having a form of godliness but denying its power. Have nothing to do with them.

What strong words Paul uses! In the original Greek, the picture that "terrible times" paints is literally one of physical or mental pain that is difficult to bear. This phrase was used in classical Greek literature to describe when one encounters dangerous wild animals, as well as raging seas.

Serious times were ahead of Timothy, both externally and, more important, from within the Church. Left and right, people would *appear* godly, but in reality would not be so (see 2 Timothy 3:5). Because of this subtle deception, it was imperative for Timothy, especially as a leader in the work, to walk in discernment, rightly understanding the times and situations in which he lives and the people he serves with.

This plea of Paul's was not just a good suggestion or something to be taken lightly. It would be crucial for Timothy—as well as each of us—to be sober-minded and understand the significance and urgency of the task, as well as the situations that influence its fulfillment, for there are enormous consequences of not living and acting with discernment.

One such illustration of these consequences is found in Joshua 9. The children of Israel were instructed by the Lord not to make treaties with any of the surrounding nations, but to destroy them and inhabit the land. The nearby Gibeonites, fearful of the reports they had heard of all that the Lord did for the children of Israel (see Joshua 9:24) and knowing that no treaty could be made with them because they were neighbors, came up with a plan to deceive the children of Israel into making a treaty with them.

> [The Gibeonites] went as a delegation whose donkeys were loaded with worn-out sacks and old wineskins, cracked and mended. The men put worn and patched sandals on their feet and wore old clothes. All the bread of their food supply was dry and moldy. Then they went to Joshua in the camp at Gilgal and

said to him and the men of Israel, "We have come from a distant country; make a treaty with us" (Joshua 9:4–6).

Joshua, not inquiring of the Lord or using discernment, made a treaty with the men, only to soon realize they were not from a distant land, but a part of those whom God had instructed them to destroy. This treaty with the Gibeonites caused a greater battle down the road for Joshua, all because he did not first act with discernment (see Joshua 10:1–4).

On the other hand, when we do walk in understanding, we are guarded by the counsel of God. Nehemiah is one such case. After being warned repeatedly by leaders opposing his work of rebuilding the wall surrounding Jerusalem, Nehemiah was told by a prophet, "Don't you know about the plot to kill you? I have a word from the Lord for you. You had better stop building the wall and take refuge in the Temple. If you don't, you're going to be killed" (paraphrase, see Nehemiah 6:10).

But Nehemiah understood that God had not sent this prophet, and he refused to believe him—"I realized that God had not sent him, but that he had prophesied against me because . . . he had been hired to intimidate me so that I would commit a sin by doing this, and then they would give me a bad name to discredit me" (Nehemiah 6:12–13).

Because Nehemiah was able to discern the genuine from the counterfeit, he came away from the situation with no harm and only greater trust in God.

Discerning Genuine from Counterfeit

"Among the gifts of the Spirit scarcely one is of greater practical usefulness than the gift of discernment. This gift should be highly valued and frankly sought as being almost indispensable in these critical times. This gift will enable us to distinguish the chaff from the wheat and to divide the manifestations of the flesh from the operations of the Spirit."[2]

The servant of God must have not just a tangible, physical understanding of the world around him, but also an understanding of the spiritual dimension. He must understand the reality of the warfare that being in the ministry assumes, and he must not go into it without discernment.

Jesus Himself gave the warning for spiritual discernment saying, "Watch out that no one deceives you. For many will come in my name, claiming, 'I am the Christ,' and will deceive many" (Matthew 24:4–5). Christianity today is full of those who look spiritual and are able to perform incredible miracles, and people, because they are of undiscerning hearts, are led astray by them.

Paul emphasizes the need for understanding by reminding Timothy of the Old Testament account of Jannes and Jambres. In Exodus 7, we see these were the men who, when Moses threw down his staff and it became a snake, Pharaoh called in as his own miracle-workers, able to perform the same things Moses did. Jannes and Jambres opposed and mocked Moses' authority and ability by imitating the miracle, trying to disprove that Moses was from God.

And just as Jannes and Jambres were esteemed by Pharaoh because of the "miracles" they could perform, so are many so-called spiritual and godly men today, when in reality some may be nothing more than counterfeits.

There are many so-called "prophets" today, running around and coming to your home, looking so godly dressed in their clean, white shirts that sparkle with holiness. Their hair is cut short, and they look well groomed. They say, "I was sleeping last night and the Lord woke me up. He gave me a vision. With my eyes wide open, you appeared before me. And the Lord spoke these words and told me I must come first thing today to deliver them to you. Glory! Glory! Glory!"

Suddenly you are trembling like a mouse that sees a cat. You think the Lord has spoken through this prophet. You assume he is a man of God and invite him in. You give him the best seat in your home and call in your wife to hear his words. But be aware that, although God still speaks today through godly men and women, some may not be sent from God at all. I have read dozens of letters about families that were destroyed and marriage relationships broken apart because of a "word from God" spoken through a "prophet."

Paul was able to uncover the truth and identify these as the godless, corrupt counterfeits they were. Nehemiah was able to see through these as well, discerning who and what was from the Lord and what was the enemy. We must be able to do the same. For we have the same kinds of wolves among us even now. Remember Paul's words in Acts 20:29–31: "Savage wolves will come in among you and will not spare the flock. Even from your own number men will arise and distort the truth in order to draw away disciples after them. So be on your guard! Remember that for three years I never stopped warning each of you night and day with tears."

We would do well to receive the exhortation from the Word of God to "believe not every spirit, but try the spirits whether they are of God: because many false prophets are gone out into the world" (1 John 4:1, KJV). Pray and ask God to give you discernment so that you will be effective in completing the task the Lord gave you and, like Nehemiah, not be swayed by the enemy's plans to deceive you and distract you from the ministry.

A Discerning Response

As participants in God's work, we can be sure we will face opposition and terrible times. It is our maturity in understanding these difficult things that determines what our response will be. If we are people of discernment, we will be able to respond by faith and in the truth of God, while those who lack understanding will be easily swayed by external circumstances and respond adversely.

We see in 2 Kings 6 an example of how spiritual understanding influenced response to difficulty. The servant of God Elisha was being hunted down by the king of Aram because he, by the Spirit of God, continually knew of the king's plans to attack Israel and would warn the people. In the night, a great army with chariots and horses was sent out to find Elisha and seize him. When Elisha's servant woke up that morning and saw they were surrounded by their enemies, he cried out with fear. But Elisha responded with faith, saying, "Don't be afraid. . . . Those who are with us are more than those who are with them" (2 Kings 6:16).

Why was Elisha able to respond like this, even when clearly surrounded by danger? It was because he was a man of understanding, able to see beyond what was happening in just the physical realm. This same understanding and discernment are what he prayed for his servant: "And Elisha prayed, 'O Lord, open his eyes so he may see.' Then the Lord opened the servant's eyes, and he looked and saw the hills full of horses and chariots of fire all around Elisha" (2 Kings 6:17).

In this, we must remember Paul's ultimate message to Timothy and take it for ourselves: *But for you, be different.* In your understanding and in your response to difficulties, be different and be one who is able to see beyond just the present circumstances and see, by faith, the truth of God and His purposes accomplished.

How to Discern

When bankers train their employees to detect counterfeit money, they do not teach them all about the characteristics of counterfeits. Rather, they teach them the characteristics of an authentic, genuine currency note, how it feels and what it looks like down to the smallest detail. Even with closed eyes, someone who has been trained well can detect the genuine from the counterfeit simply by the way it feels in his hand.

It takes the grace of God and the power of the Holy Spirit for us to understand things that are beyond our sight, hearing and natural perception. People can easily look spiritual, talk the same language and modify their behavior according to the expectation required of them, appearing as an "angel of light" and deceiving the people of God. This is the reason why every believer, especially those who are in some form of leadership within the ministry, must be very sensitive to be able to discern between the two.

How do we begin to do this? Simply put, a "tree is recognized by its own fruit" (Luke 6:44).

Please do not misunderstand—this fruit of which Jesus spoke does not refer to the activities of ministry but rather the overflow of one's inner life, as described in Galatians 5:22–24, also known as the fruit of the Holy Spirit: "When the Holy Spirit controls our lives, he will produce this kind of fruit in us: love, joy, peace, patience, kindness, goodness, faithfulness, gentleness, and self-control" (NLT). When this fruit is not present, it is an indicator that something within is not right, even if the person is involved in full-time ministry and holds a lot of responsibilities.

Every single one of the characteristics that Paul tells Timothy to be aware of are fruits of the flesh rather than the Spirit: "People will be lovers of themselves, lovers of money, boastful, proud, abusive, disobedient to their parents, ungrateful, unholy, without love, unforgiving, slanderous, without self-control, brutal, not lovers of the good, treacherous, rash, conceited, lovers of pleasure rather than lovers of God—having a form of godliness but denying its power" (2 Timothy 3:2–5).

That is quite a list! Notice that of the 18 expressions Paul uses to describe the kind of people, the moral conditions and the dangerous social climate that Timothy would be dealing with, they are all sandwiched between two phrases—*"lovers of themselves"* and *"lovers of pleasure rather than lovers of God."*

From this, we can conclude then that the fundamental problem was rooted in misdirected love. Instead of being lovers of God first and foremost, they became lovers of self and lovers of pleasure, which overflowed and infected every part of their character and behavior. But when a person abides in Christ, he will bring forth the fruit of the Spirit out of his pure heart that loves and seeks the Lord (see John 15).

Again, it all has to do with the fruit of our lives, not the activities of the ministry. If a person's life is not manifesting the life of Jesus in all His humility, brokenness, love, dependence upon the Father and compassion, that is a good indicator that his inner life is polluted with self-love and the love of pleasure.

A Warning

Instead of trying to analyze all the many problems and difficulties that we deal with, we must be careful not to fall into the trap of loving ourselves and our righteousness so much that we become the judge of our brother or sister.

Remember that our Lord who told us to test the spirits also said,

> Do not judge, or you too will be judged. For in the same way
> you judge others, you will be judged, and with the measure you

use, it will be measured to you. Why do you look at the speck of sawdust in your brother's eye and pay no attention to the plank in your own eye? How can you say to your brother, "Let me take the speck out of your eye," when all the time there is a plank in your own eye? You hypocrite, first take the plank out of your own eye, and then you will see clearly to remove the speck from your brother's eye (Matthew 7:1–5).

Paul even went as far to say that he didn't even judge himself (see 1 Corinthians 4:3). Therefore, our response to people whose attitude and life do not match up with the fruit of the Holy Spirit must be one of concern for them, out of love and mercy. We must be loving, yet all the while careful of how we fellowship with them, for we are told to "have nothing to do with them" (2 Timothy 3:5).

Endure to the End

How true it is today that just as Timothy was called to face difficult times and lead God's work, we are faced with the same task. Jesus said that "because of the increase of wickedness, the love of most will grow cold" (Matthew 24:12). But Jesus didn't end it there. He challenged us, encouraged us, that even so, "he who stands firm to the end will be saved" (Matthew 24:13).

We must ask ourselves what was Christ meaning when He said this. He who stands firm in what? In hard work? In sacrifice? In knowledge? In a discerning spirit? No, *in love.* He who endures in love will stand firm until the end—love not for self or for pleasure, but for God and for others. For it is by our love that we will be identified as His (see John 13:35).

If Timothy had to face these kinds of deceivers and counterfeits in the first century, we can only imagine the kind of deception that we are dealing with in our generation. The only safeguard that we have in this is to stay in intimate relationship with the Lord Jesus Christ and follow Him closely, hungering to become like Him in every area of our lives. By this, we will be protected from going astray ourselves, and we will know the real and authentic One so closely that discernment will come easily and be handled with love and concern.

Do not be unwise but of a discerning heart, able to determine what is the good and perfect will of God.

sixteen

the power
of influence

When I was 16 years old, just a frail, shy boy, I heard George Verwer speak near my village about having a radical commitment to Christ and a passion for lost souls. The Lord used that incident and the example of George Verwer's life and passion to set me on the road that later led me to surrender my whole life for full-time ministry.

In the years after that experience, George Verwer became more and more influential in my life and walk with the Lord. I spent eight years serving with his organization, preaching the Gospel all over India. It was his life and ministry that became my example of what it means to genuinely and humbly walk with and serve the Lord. And even now, 35 years later, he is still my example. To this day, I can tell you that when I have some decision to make, I think to myself, *What kind of decision would George make in this situation?* Although my decisions may be different than his because our organizations are different, I use the example of his life and ministry to help guide my thinking.

Now, by the grace of God, I have at least half a dozen other people in different areas of kingdom work whose lives I follow as I seek to serve the Lord, patterning my life after theirs.

This principle of having an example to follow is what Paul was communicating in 2 Timothy 3:10–11 when he said to Timothy,

> You, however, know all about my teaching, my way of life, my purpose, faith, patience, love, endurance, persecutions, sufferings—what kinds of things happened to me in Antioch, Iconium and Lystra, the persecutions I endured.

Paul is calling Timothy to remember the example that he has been for him in the ministry through the way he lived his life. *Timothy, you have seen my life. You have known firsthand the kind of man that I am, the example I have set. You know all that I've endured, the way I have loved and persevered, the things I have taught and the faith by which I have lived.*

Why is this so significant to point out? Because, as I mentioned in Chapter 8, we are in desperate need today for men and women of God who can say to younger believers, just as Paul said to Timothy, *You have seen my life. You know my example. Follow me as I follow Christ.*

This is especially significant for the time that Paul is saying these things to Timothy. Paul's journey was long and hard, and soon Timothy would be entering into an even greater battle. From his years of experience in the ministry, Paul knew that Timothy would not be able to make it on his own—no servant of God can. He would need to remember Paul's example to aid him in fulfilling the ministry.

We, too, need men and women in our lives whom we can look to as godly examples, helping us fulfill the call God has placed upon us. Even though you may be anointed like Moses, Joshua or David, you will not be able to handle things all on your own. We need people whose lives help serve as a guide-post along our journey. We must not become independent, becoming our own counsel, measuring standard or judge. By keeping good examples in your life, people who will correct you and encourage you, you ensure that you will continue to run well the race that you began.

Paul was this kind of example to Timothy, and we see how he found this model in ministry from Jesus Himself. From the very beginning of His ministry, Jesus set an example for His disciples to follow, calling them to come to Him and learn from His life (see Matthew 11:29). And they in turn, when Jesus had ascended, remembered how He had lived, followed in His foot-steps and set the example for future disciples to follow.

This is how the kingdom of God works: We must have an example whom we can follow as we serve the Lord, and we, in turn, must become the kind of example others can follow in their walks with the Lord.

The Plumb Line

There is a simple yet incredibly important device that masons use when building—the plumb line. The plumb line is a cord from which a weight is suspended, enabling them to rightly determine an absolutely perfect line by which to build. Brick is laid only after a precise line has been determined with this device, for if they do not follow an absolutely straight line when building, the wall will be crooked and will not stand long.

No matter how good or experienced a mason may be, he never builds by the judgment of his own eye—he always uses the plumb line. It is not used just once either; there is a constant checking of each brick with the plumb line. Even if a brick is just one centimeter off from the plumb line, it must be removed and replaced until it is perfectly straight.

In our walk with the Lord, the lives of trusted men and women of God (along with the Word of God) serve as our plumb line, keeping us on the straight and narrow road, serving as a standard by which to continually measure our lives and ministry against. By this, we ensure that we are on the right course and build well.

In 2 Timothy 3:10–14, Paul lays down the plumb line of his own life for Timothy to follow as he carries on the work after he is gone, pointing out various aspects of his life as a ruler for Timothy, an example for him to pattern his own life and ministry by. Paul then reminds Timothy of all the kinds of things that happened to him:

> [You know] what kinds of things happened to me in Antioch, Iconium and Lystra, the persecutions I endured. Yet the Lord rescued me from all of them. In fact, everyone who wants to live a godly life in Christ Jesus will be persecuted, while evil men and impostors will go from bad to worse, deceiving and being deceived. But as for you, continue in what you have learned and have become convinced of, because you know those from whom you learned it, and how from infancy you have known the holy Scriptures, which are able to make you wise for salvation through faith in Christ Jesus (2 Timothy 3:11–15).

Paul continues, saying, *Timothy, all of this stuff will continue to go on all around you. But remember the example you have seen in me. Remember the lives of those you have learned the Scriptures from and pattern your life accordingly.* In a day when evil men and imposters in the church increase, Timothy must be sure to follow those who are genuinely godly, who have demonstrated through their character and their choices, over a long period of time, the kind of person they are—rather than just following men who have the form of godliness but deny the power (see 2 Timothy 3:5). These, although they may look and sound good, are imposters.

Even today, we must receive this same plea. Christendom is filled with many who are absolute phonies, having no reality of the life of Christ, and who are just out to make money and build a name for themselves.

This is the reason I want to highlight one specific area in which Paul tells Timothy to follow him—the purpose that Paul lived for: "You, however, know . . . my purpose" (2 Timothy 3:10). *Timothy, you know what I live for.* Everything about Paul's life declared his purpose. There was no mistaking it—it permeated all that he did and the man he was, and it was a sure, solid model for Timothy.

I will never forget, as a young man hardly 18 years old, serving the Lord in Bombay with Operation Mobilization. One morning, a skinny English man met with the 70 of us serving in that city during our morning prayer meeting before we went out into the streets to distribute tracts. I will never forget his statement. With an urgency in his eyes, he said, "My brothers, last night I was on the top of this seven-story building. As I looked down upon Bombay, a city always like day because it never sleeps, I saw people flowing through the streets like a rushing river. And I broke down and wept for God to touch this city." Then, with the same urgency and passion, he said, "Let's go and distribute Gospel tracts."

I had two shoulder bags filled with tracts. George Verwer, who had made that statement, slung his own two bags over both shoulders and set out with all of us. We were thrust out into the streets of Bombay distributing tracts from morning until late at night. Periodically, a truck would come by and keep filling our bags with more tracts. As the day wore on, my nose began to bleed, as I had not had enough food—not even enough to drink—but we could not stop. I just kept seeing that skinny English man standing before some Indians, weeping his eyes out for the people in Bombay going to hell and joining with us all day long, in the heat, to distribute Gospel tracts.

How can you forget such a man? What he said and what he did were one, they were united, and as with Paul, it was clear to see the purpose for which he lived. So it must be for those we follow and for our lives as well.

Interesting, isn't it, how not just one or two examples but the whole lifestyle of a person portrays his purpose in life? Everything in the life of a businessman whose goal is to become a millionaire—his conversations, his decisions, his opinions, the things he reads, the way he spends his time and all his plans—all demonstrate the purpose for which he lives. So it is in the life of a servant of God. His relationships and choices, his very household—his children, their habits and their behavior—all portray the purpose of his life. Ministry is not just a job he carries out on the weekdays from 9 to 5. No, it is his way of life, his purpose. And it sets the example for younger believers to follow.

Let us all live lives that pave the way for others to follow. Can you who are called to serve the King of kings and the Lord of lords and to reach a continent of billions going to hell tell a younger brother or sister with whom you serve, "You know the purpose of my life; study me and follow me as I follow Christ"? Or when that younger brother or sister watches you, does he or she see only that you want a two-wheeler, a car, a better house or new clothes? What is *your* purpose? Every servant of God should be able to lead others with the example of their life and purpose.

How often do you use the plumb line of another's example

and of the Word of God? Once in the morning? In the evening? No, if you don't use it throughout your day, by evening your wall will be crooked. It may be only two or three degrees off, but when it is no longer straight, ultimately the whole building will collapse. Let us build our lives after the truth of the Word of God and the solid example of genuine, godly men and women.

What Kind of Model to Look For

Do you have a model you can follow, as Timothy had Paul? I encourage you to find someone in the ministry whose life and example you can imitate. You see, rules, regulations, seminars and books on how to live and serve God can go only so far in helping us. We are creatures who, from infancy, learn by example, imitating what we see in others.

For this reason, who you choose is a very important decision. Please, refuse to look up to any Christian leader who is not manifesting the life of Jesus—His kind of love, commitment, sacrifice and humility. There are many superstar religious leaders who are looked up to because of the "anointing," their ability to draw big crowds and a lot of money. But these are not the requirements shown in the Bible as godly models. We must follow those who are broken and humble, those whose inner life and outer life are in agreement and who manifest the life of Jesus and the fruit of the Spirit.

In our following of godly men and women, we must also keep in mind that they are still human. They will not be perfect, but if they are godly, we can follow their example. Even in the Bible, God paints the lives of His heroes in a frank way that exposes their failures and tragedies. Why? Because by revealing their flaws, God is saying, "I am the God not of perfect people, but holy people." It is interesting to note, for example, that God never says, "I am the God of Abraham, Isaac and Israel." Instead He says, over and over again, "I am the God of Abraham, Isaac and *Jacob.*" Although God changed Jacob's name to *Israel,* meaning "prince of God," the Lord still identifies Himself as "the God of Jacob"—the God of a flawed man. Even with my following George Verwer's example, I often tell people, "He is not a perfect man, but he is the man to whom I first submitted my life, saying, 'He is my leader.' "

Until you find a tangible model to follow, read the stories of saints who have gone before you, like the biography of Sadhu Sundar Singh or stories from the Bible. For example, if you are a sister, you can read about Amy Carmichael, Pandita Ramabai or Mother Teresa. It is not that everything they did was correct or that you should do things exactly the way they did. But at least you can see the principles by which they operated. Model your life after theirs, learning from the experiences they had and the way they responded to life.

"Follow Me . . ."

I urge you to not only find someone whose life example you can follow and whose purpose is known, but also seek to become the kind of person another can follow. This is the true and most influential leadership—our lives.

When my son was four years old, our family went to visit some brothers who minister by the seashore in Kanniyakumari on the other side of Trivandrum. One morning, I decided to take a walk on the beach before the day began. I rolled up my *doti* and walked in the wet sand, deliberately leaving the impression of my feet. As I was walking along, I heard someone behind me. I looked back and saw my son. Do you know what he was doing? He was following my footsteps. Quietly I said to myself, *O God, please help me. He is saying, "When I grow up, I want to be just like you."*

The same thing will happen to you. When your daughter grows up, she will say, "I want to be just like my mommy." When your son grows up, he will say, "I want to be just like my daddy." The young Bible college student will say, "I want to be just like my teacher." The coworker just assigned to the mission field will say, "I want to be just like my mentor." Are you comfortable with that? Paul was. He had no shame, no arrogance and no fear. He loved Timothy and had invested his life in him and could say confidently, "Timothy, you follow me as I follow Christ. Don't worry about all the struggles, problems, difficulties, misunderstandings, letdowns or pain. Your call is a mighty, awesome call. Follow in my footsteps."

Peter emphasizes this point of leading by example when he speaks to those who are in leadership in the Body of Christ, telling them to "[not lord] over those entrusted to you, but being examples to the flock" (1 Peter 5:3). Whatever responsibility God has given you and whatever people are working with you or you are responsible for, your call is not to be a tyrant, not to make demands, saying, "Do this!" or "Do that!" but to be a living example to others, caring for and leading them as Jesus did with His disciples. People will naturally want to follow you because of the kind of life you lead. It was what Timothy saw in Paul's life and the person he was that stirred within him the desire to become like and follow him. Our example is not seen in the things we say or just the way we act in public—we lead with our lives and with our love. As Paul said, "What you have seen in me, do. Then you can teach someone else what I have taught you" (paraphrase, see 2 Thessalonians 3:7, 9). This principle of leading by example is what the kingdom of God and this ministry are built on.

If you destroy the very foundation of the ministry in which you work, how can you cultivate the next generation of young people so they are willing to give their own lives to go places for Jesus' sake where no one has ever gone before? If you cannot say, "Follow me," you are like a man who climbs a tree, sits on a branch, then turns around and chops off the very branch on which he is sitting.

I would like you to think along with me and ask yourself, *Am I a model to others in these things as I work for the Lord?* Consider these areas of life: optimism, diplomacy, work ethics, self-control, love and compassion. How am I setting an example in obedience, the way I use my tongue and the way I respond to difficulties, failure, jealousy and loneliness? Am I a good example in being attentive, humble, content and courageous? How is my neatness, time management, reverence, discipline, forgiveness, gratefulness, dependability, patience, determination, loyalty, endurance, hospitality, sincerity, generosity, flexibility, enthusiasm and punctuality? Am I a good example when it comes to discernment, living by faith, alertness, having a mind to suffer, resourcefulness, responsibility, delegation, tolerance, creativity, joyfulness, sensitivity, wisdom and thoroughness? How is my burden for the lost? Do I set a good example in stewardship, handling money, comforting others and how to live with vision and handle ambition? Do I take initiative? Am I able to set the example of how to listen, communicate, disciple others and encourage?

Strengthening the Kingdom

Let us remember that at the point that Paul was writing these words to Timothy, his time on earth was just about over. *I lived every day as though it was the best day and the last day,* he was saying. *I invested my life faithfully, and you are one of those individuals in whom I invested it, to help build the kingdom of God.* In closing, Paul tells Timothy to "continue in what you have learned and have become convinced of, because you know those from whom you learned it" (2 Timothy 3:14). From infancy Timothy has known the holy Scriptures, has now seen them lived out by Paul's example, and if he continues in these things, then he will be thoroughly equipped for every good work (see 2 Timothy 3:15–17).

And so will we, if we continue on following the godly models we have before us. A brother called by the Lord and willing to internalize this radical reality will survive until the very end.

I want you to imagine that tomorrow afternoon by five o'clock your life will be over. What do you want to leave behind when you say goodbye to everything here? Commit yourself with this burden: "Lord, I want to be that individual who, when my journey comes to an end and I am lying on my deathbed, my last hours drawing nigh, can look back over my life and see hundreds of young people going on to serve You and building Your kingdom because of the example I have been and the life I have led." By the grace of God, may this be true of you and me.

We are influencing and being influenced all the time. Walk wisely.

seventeen

call to evangelism

I will never forget when I was a young boy growing up in my village. It was summertime, the harvest was over and the days were spent flying kites with my friends in the fields beside our village. There had not been rain for many weeks, and it was extremely hot. As we were flying our kites one day, we saw a thatched-roof house go up in flames about a furlong from where we stood. Smoke billowed and flames shot up to the sky, and then we heard a terrible scream. Never before or since have I heard anything so terrifying. I will never forget it.

The scream came from a mother whose baby boy was asleep in the burning house. Her scream was so loud and urgent that all of us boys started screaming too. We did not know what else to do. Others from my village came frantically running toward the burning home to rescue the little boy.

Fortunately, the boy was rescued, and today he is an engineer in Cochin.

Even to this day, I can go back to that memory, hearing once again the terrifying screams of that mother for her child on the brink of death. I can still sense the urgency with which the men in my village ran with all their might to rescue the child from the burning hut. And it is with this same desperate urgency that Paul speaks to Timothy one of his strongest statements yet, found in 2 Timothy 4:1–2:

> In the presence of God and of Christ Jesus, who will judge the living and the dead, and in view of his appearing and his kingdom, I give you this charge: Preach the Word.

In the Greek, the word *charge* is *diamarturomai*. It is an especially strong word, having the weight of a legal affirmation and meaning to testify under oath in a court of law.

Although Paul could have spent his last few sentences talking about a thousand things, instead he used this last opportunity of his to communicate how overcome with desperation he was because of so many lost souls and the need to reach them with the Gospel. He resorted to phrases and words he used nowhere else in his writings. He could not have been speaking more forcefully than when he wrote, "Preach the Word" and "Do the work of an evangelist" (2 Timothy 4:2, 5). Paul's most important message to Timothy and what all his instruction led up to was this one thing: Reach the lost.

The Reason for It All

You see, the essence of the whole Christian life, the reason for which the living God became a man and died on the cross, was for the purpose of redemption: "For God so loved the world . . ." (John 3:16). The only reason God has kept us on this earth is to be witnesses to Him, joining Him in the work of seeing the spiritually dead come to eternal life through Jesus.

Our one purpose is this: to somehow, some way, win the lost at all costs and prepare them for the coming of the Lord.

When you look at the village or district in which you work—the low caste, the high caste, the slum-dwellers, the Muslims or the Dalits—close your eyes and see, by faith, that these hundred million or more people are those for whom Christ died, called to be disciples of Jesus and destined to reign with Him forever.

Let us then live and work in such a way that one day they will be in the fold, in your church even! Let your intention be to see them come to know Jesus Christ. Just as Paul told Timothy to do the work right now, so must you. Paul, with deep conviction and urgency, told Timothy a lot about the call placed upon him as a servant of God. He spoke much about the responsibility, the way to handle the ministry, instructing him in various situations and offering warnings for down the road. But everything that Paul spoke of led up to this one thing—preach the Gospel. It was the purpose of everything.

You see, learning is not good enough. Being is not good enough. Knowing is not good enough. Paul is saying, *Timothy, you must take what you've learned, what you know, what you've seen in me and the person you've become and now you must preach the Gospel, make it known, proclaim it!* And it is the same for us! The Greek word Paul used here for "preach" literally describes someone who, representing a higher authority, goes into the marketplace shouting at the top of his lungs to make his announcement known. It is this passionate pursuit to reach the lost that is the true indicator of an authentic, godly, Christlike life.

All Are Called

There are many today who go around claiming, "God has called me for a special ministry of teaching." It sounds wonderful when they say, "My gifting is to be a prophet," or "I am an apostle," or they claim some other calling. But when the house is on fire, do they scream out for help and go running to rescue the perishing? No, instead they say, "The house is on fire and people are dying, but I am not called to be the fireman to rescue them."

I have great difficulty with people who say good things with their lips but demonstrate no feeling or pain for the lost and dying millions going to hell. The whole Bible, from start to finish, is about redemption, revealing the Savior of mankind—Jesus Christ, who came only "to seek and to save that which was lost" (Luke 19:10). I wonder what is behind their reasoning. Is it that they think themselves more important than Jesus, more able than He, a better teacher, prophet and miracle worker? Do they think themselves better than the disciples of Jesus?

Why am I saying that? In the Gospels, you can clearly see for yourself what Jesus was all about—reaching the lost. If you think you are such a special, anointed teacher or prophet, please know you are missing the mark, the whole reason Jesus came and called us to serve Him. Jesus, the greatest of all teachers, was a soul-winner (see Matthew 9:35). He came to preach the Good News and set the captives free. Why, then, is it that there are those in the Church who reason away not carrying a few Gospel tracts and handing them to the people they pass every day, people who don't know Jesus?

Then, consider this as well: What was the first thing Jesus told His disciples when He called them? "Come, follow me,… and I will make you *fishers of men*" (Mark 1:17, emphasis mine). And what was the last thing He told them? "Go and make disciples . . ." (see Matthew 28:19). After this, when the Holy Spirit was given as promised, all was for the furtherance of the Gospel. Everything started, continued and propelled toward this one end—to reach the lost! How we must be about our Father's business!

No matter what gift you may have, what position, title, ministry, how high or low a position, what temperament you are or if you're in full-time ministry or not, we have no excuse for not witnessing to the great salvation of God. Acts 8:4 shows us that evangelism is not just for full-time workers, but for *every child of God.*

Timothy was timid by temperament and young by age, yet he must preach the Gospel and do the work of an evangelist nonetheless, always fulfilling all the duties of his ministry.

Because of this, because we are called to follow in His footsteps, our purpose must be the same. We must keep away from the trap of pursuing a deeper life and forgetting the purpose for all spiritual knowledge and gifts. What I am trying to say is that the closer you come to Jesus, the more your godliness becomes a reality. Does anyone have a deeper life than Jesus Himself? The more you understand God's ways, the more your heart will become like that of Jesus, broken for the lost and dying millions all around you.

Whatever your calling, when the house is on fire, will you do something about it? Even if you do nothing, will you at least shout, "Somebody, please come; people are dying in the house"?

Whatever It Takes

Hell is a reality.

There is a fixed time for sinful man to find salvation in Jesus Christ. When that time has passed, those without salvation are lost forever, damned to hell for eternity. Our finite minds cannot grasp the reality of eternity, let alone eternity in hell. There is no relief to look forward to—for all eternity, these lost people will scream at the top of their lungs engulfed in flames, "Please give me a drop of water!" But there is no water. So they scream out, "All I want is to die! Just let me die!" But there is no death for them either.

Paul understood this. That is why he wrote such strong words, willing to give his own life just to see people saved. In Romans 9:1–4 (paraphrase), speaking of the Jewish people, he says, "If it were possible to save my own people by cutting my throat and letting my blood pour out, I would do it. I would do anything if it were possible somehow, somewhere, some way, to pull even a few out of the flames." And it is why, even when sitting in prison, he wrote, "I rejoice about all that has happened to me, even this terrible imprisonment, because it is helping spread the Gospel" (paraphrase, see Philippians 1:12–14). He said that he would "endure everything for the sake of the elect, that they too may obtain the salvation that is in Christ Jesus, with eternal glory" (2 Timothy 2:10).

Who are the elect of our day, those for whom, just like Paul, we must endure all things, giving everything just to tell them about Jesus? They are the most unreached, those living in the high mountains and valleys of Nepal—the poor, broken, destitute, crying, dying lepers and children across India; all those across the world who have never heard of God, heaven, hell or even the name *Jesus;* those who do not know there is a Bible. Millions like these men and women today are the elect. God knows and loves them. They need to hear the Good News about Jesus' love and salvation before it is too late.

Hear Paul's words again and remember who it is saying

them: "I endure everything for the sake of the elect." Paul, the son of a rich man, born into a high and elite family—enduring imprisonment and brutal beatings, for the sake of telling people about Jesus. Paul, the Jewish scholar and former member of the ruling Sanhedrin—enduring nakedness, hunger and shipwreck, just to travel to that small village to preach the Gospel. Paul, theologian and philosopher, once respected in his day—now enduring floggings and being chased out of town. Why? Because a passion for the lost consumed him and drove him from town to town all to preach the Gospel no matter what the cost.

God is looking for the same type of commitment and passion from us today. No matter where we came from, what we may have done in the past or how high in worldly standards we have ascended, it's all worthless. Like Paul, and like our Savior, no matter who we are, we must be willing to endure all things for the sake of even just a few coming to know the saving power and love of Jesus Christ.

The Power of the Gospel

May our hearts be gripped with this purpose, just as it gripped Timothy's young heart. Paul was saying, "Timothy, don't sit quietly. Reach out! Times are difficult. Persecution is here. I am in prison and am going to be killed very soon. But don't you stop! Don't come to the place where you care only about training, about having a deeper life or about worshiping and learning more and more. No, Timothy, get out and do the work of evangelism, winning people to Christ and making disciples."

Brothers and sisters, I say the same to you today. Maybe you are reading this in Bible college right now. Maybe you are on a mission field somewhere. Maybe the Lord has placed you as a teacher or you are working in some business. Whatever you may do and wherever you may be, please understand that the purpose of all that the Lord has invested in your life is to see you join in His great ultimate purpose of soul winning. This is the highest of all calls.

Rescue the perishing.

eighteen

determined to finish

Knowing the desperate seriousness of Timothy's responsibility, especially in light of Paul's imminent death, the aged mentor once again brings his own personal commitment and life as an example for his beloved son to follow—"I have fought the good fight, I have finished the race, I have kept the faith" (2 Timothy 4:7). Paul reminds Timothy to stay sober and endure all things so that he might finish the race set before him.

It is interesting that Paul likened the spiritual life to that of a race. And, as we all know, no one starts out a race to stop halfway through and drink a cup of tea. No marathon runner, after training for months and miles on end, has in his heart to quit running after 13 miles and go home to sleep. No, his intention is to run the full 26 miles and complete the race. Even if he meets hardship on the way, even if his body aches and his muscles cramp, he is determined to press on until he reaches the finish line.

This element of persistence is of great importance in the life of the servant of God as well. Like the marathon runner, many difficulties, hardships and disappointments will come our way as we run the race set before us. Loved ones will misunderstand us, opposition will beat upon us, loneliness may surround us and trials may seem to be on our every side. In the midst of these, it is only the inner resolve to persist to the end that will keep us pressing on no matter what. And it is this determination to finish that regulates everything we do.

Determination is like a sharp knife, able to cut through all the things that may cloud or block the way before us. It has eyes to see past these momentary difficulties to the great reward at the end. And it is this characteristic alone—no matter who you are or how your race started—that differentiates between those who reach the goal and those who do not.

It's How You Finish

Notice, however, that the word *determination* connotes over a period of time. It's being in it for the long haul. Determination in no way speaks of just starting well. Rather, it speaks of the end result, of *finishing* well. This is what Paul was trying to communicate to Timothy.

You see, Paul had seen many come and go in his day, many who had started well but who eventually began to "seek their own" (Philippians 2:21, NKJV) and, because of it, never finished their race. Demas, his former colaborer in the ministry, was just one of them.

The Bible gives numerous examples of men like this. Solomon, the son of the great King David, started out his reign with a sincere heart, asking God not for riches or power but for wisdom. "The Lord was pleased that Solomon had asked for this" (1 Kings 3:10) and, because of his request, not only gave him wisdom, but also added riches and power on top of it.

From just this passage, Solomon can appear to be headed in the right direction. Indeed, he was, but the right direction means nothing if you do not reach your destination. This is precisely what happened with Solomon. He ended up a broken man who chased after the wind, lamenting over the loss of all. He who started out requesting wisdom ended up calling it all meaningless (see Ecclesiastes 1:16–17).

Samson is another man who started out well but did not reach the end. Even with an incredible anointing and ministry given to him by God, he did not complete his race (see Judges 15–16). Judas, one of Christ's disciples, started very well, yet along the way he *became* a betrayer. Gehazi, the disciple of Elisha, had every possibility of becoming the next mighty prophet of God, yet his greed overtook him and he became a leper.

In the New Testament, we see that Jesus had more than just the 12 disciples that most are familiar with. There were hundreds who followed Him, yet not all of them endured to the end. When life became tough or they did not understand what Jesus was doing or saying, they stopped following Him (see John 6:60).

Today, the story continues. Hundreds of thousands proclaim that they want Jesus, forgiveness of sins and to go to heaven. Many say they want to give their lives to serve Him, but then, as opposition comes and they face misunderstanding, scorning and persecution, many fall away. What was it that hindered these men and so many of us today from reaching the goal? What kept them and what keeps us from finishing the race?

Keeping Sight

The reasons can be many but are often traced back to this one—*losing sight*. Somewhere along the way, these saints forgot what was before them, the reason they began in the first place, and within time, the race is forfeited. When we fail to fix our eyes on Jesus and instead begin to put our focus on ourselves, our circumstances and others, our step begins to slow, and before we even realize it, we can be on our way out of the race.

It is for that reason Hebrews 12:2–3 exhorts and reminds us to "fix our eyes on Jesus, the author and perfecter of our faith, who for the joy set before him endured the cross, scorning its shame, and sat down at the right hand of the throne of God. Consider him who endured such opposition from sinful men, so that you will not grow weary and lose heart."

You see, Jesus is our "forerunner" (Hebrews 6:20, NKJV), or example. Christ has gone before us, showing us how to live on this earth. He knew the pain and difficulty that this life contains, and He, too, had to press through it all until He reached the goal set before Him. Throughout Christ's life there were numerous temptations and serious attacks from the powers of darkness to keep Him from reaching His goal of the cross. Satan tried his best to hinder Jesus, even attempting to kill Him as an infant (see Matthew 2).

All throughout His ministry, there was the temptation to make compromises (see Matthew 4). But Jesus refused to give in, even when experiencing incredible hunger, weariness and despair. He was determined to reach the goal. Even up to the hours before He would make that fatal, triumphant journey to the cross, He was presented with opportunities that would make His road easier, but He kept His focus. He endured to the end.

From His example we gain the fortitude and strength to press on. "For we do not have a high priest who is unable to sympathize with our weaknesses, but we have one who has been tempted in every way, just as we are" (Hebrews 4:15).

My brothers and sisters, our path will not be easy. It will be difficult at times. Even so, we must keep our eyes on Jesus—the Author and Finisher of our faith—and press on until we reach the end. This is what Paul did, and because of it he was able to say:

> I have fought the good fight, I have finished the race, I have kept the faith. Now there is in store for me the crown of righteousness, which the Lord, the righteous Judge, will award to me on that day—and not only to me, but also to all who have longed for his appearing (2 Timothy 4:7–8).

What an accomplishment to be able to say, "I have finished the race." It has been completed. I have accomplished the task given to me. How? By keeping sight of Jesus.

Incentive to Endure

Because Paul kept sight of Jesus, we read how he also "longed for His appearing." I believe it was the reality of Christ coming for him, the burning desire in Paul's heart to be with Him, that also put strength in his step and kept him pressing on. Read through the book of Acts, and you will see the wide variety of intense troubles Paul had along his journey. Even so, he confidently declared that these "light and momentary troubles are achieving for us an eternal glory that far outweighs them all. So we fix our eyes not on what is seen, but on what is unseen. For what is seen is temporary, but what is unseen is eternal" (2 Corinthians 4:17–18). With hope and anticipation in his heart, he longed for Jesus' return and pressed on.

In fact, Paul confessed to the believers in Philippi that he'd rather be with the Lord than with them (see Philippians 3). It was this longing that enabled him to throw off all the things that would try to deter him from his goal. Those who have this hope of one day seeing Jesus purify themselves of all that hinders, staying on the narrow road no matter what.

Are you someone who longs for His appearing? This hope we have—of one day seeing and being with Jesus—is our greatest incentive to endure.

Unfortunately, it is all too easy for many of us to lose touch with this promise of God—He *is* soon coming for us. "Let not your heart be troubled. . . . I will come again and receive you to Myself; that where I am, there you may be also" (John 14:1, 3, NKJV). We often forget this hope we have and the victory and joy that await us and, therefore, set up camp where we are and no longer press forward.

One year for my birthday, Bob, a dear brother who served the Lord with us, gave me a copy of a painting that now hangs on the wall in my study. The scene is from after the Rapture, and Jesus is now embracing one of His followers. As you look at it, you are drawn to the believer, kind of weary and tired, worn-out from the long battle, and now slumping over Jesus' shoulder. There's a sense of peace and security about it, as well as a sense of relief and fulfillment, as Jesus holds the weary man in His arms. He has made it. Finally, he has made it.

As I look at the picture, it is as though the Lord is saying, "I waited so long to see you. I know you are tired. It's been a long journey, and the battle was rough. Many times you felt like giving up—and many have. But you pressed on! Welcome home, my child!"

Every time I see this portrait, my heart longs even more for the day when I will see Him face to face. Bob, the dear brother who gave me this gift, is seeing Him face to face. He went to be with the Lord in 2001.

This expectant hope is the key for our lives. The battle is tough and long, but my brothers and sisters, it is momentary! And it doesn't compare even slightly to the great joy and rest that await us, when we will be embraced in the strong, everlasting arms of our Savior. He is able to carry us through, if only we don't give up. May our prayer ever be, "Maranatha! Come, Lord Jesus, come."

Fix your eyes on the things that are unseen like Abraham did (Hebrews 11), and you will find the strength to press on.

We Must Choose

Paul fought the good fight. *He* made the choice to get up over and over again, after numerous beatings, shipwrecks and disasters, to keep fighting. Yes, God calls and He gives grace, yet our responsibility remains. If we want to win, we have to fight. If we want the crown, we have to run until we reach the finish line.

This is what Paul did. His was not a careless, "if it is convenient" kind of commitment. No. He was determined, so much so that he said, "I consider my life worth nothing to me, if only I may finish the race and complete the task the Lord Jesus has given me—the task of testifying to the gospel of God's grace" (Acts 20:24). This one thing was on his mind—to finish the race.

We must take heed and understand the reality of our enemy, the one who prowls around like a roaring lion, seeking who he can devour.

You see, the enemy's tools are subtle. If he can't stop you from starting the race and battle, he will do all he can to take you out somewhere in the *middle* of it. There are hundreds of reasons why people don't survive in this race. As you read these lines, the Holy Spirit will remind you of things in your own life of which you need to be careful so that you finish the race you began. Think where you may be in the next 5 or 10 years. Determine now that no matter what comes along, nothing will move you or hinder you from finishing the race the Lord Jesus called you to.

You may be called to be a teacher of God's Word. Another is called to be a leader or administrator. Someone else is called to be an evangelist or an apostle, pioneering church-planting work in unreached areas. Perhaps you are called to be a servant and assist others or to be a support to someone who is leading the way. Maybe God has called you to be an encourager like Barnabas and hold up the arms of another. Whatever that call may be, it is most important that you choose to keep going even in the face of adversity and press on toward the mark.

As Calvin Coolidge once said, "Press on. Nothing in the world can take the place of persistence. Talent will not; nothing is more common than unsuccessful individuals with talent. Genius will not; unrewarded genius is almost a proverb. Education will not; the world is full of educated derelicts. Persistence and determination alone are omnipotent."[1]

In his last words, Paul uses that charge once more—*but for you*—saying, "Timothy, many people may deny the faith, many may grow weary and tired and step out of the race, but for you, persist to the end. Crisis is everywhere and there will be times when you are tempted to say, 'I need a break!' but remember, I am no longer there to help hold things together. It is now up to you. You must remain strong to oversee the work, to counsel others and to do the work yourself, despite the hardships you face."

Don't give up. Keep pressing on toward the goal.

nineteen

suffering loss

Paul's tone of voice seems to shift in the last chapter of his letter to Timothy. No more is he giving direct instruction and counsel, and in no other place are Paul's humanity and pain in the ministry revealed more than in his closing words:

> Do your best to come to me quickly, for Demas, because he loved this world, has deserted me and has gone to Thessalonica. Crescens has gone to Galatia, and Titus to Dalmatia. Only Luke is with me. . . . At my first defense, no one came to my support, but everyone deserted me (2 Timothy 4:9–12, 16).

You can almost hear the pain in Paul's voice as he asks Timothy to please come quickly. Why? Because he has been left all alone. Here is the great apostle Paul, now shut up in a prison awaiting his death sentence. All the years he suffered, the months he gave to travel stormy seas so that he could build up and encourage the Church, all the letters he's written, all the persecution he endured—all now to have everyone desert him.

These were not just ordinary men that left him, but his fellow workers in the ministry, those who had shared in the victory and trials of the kingdom's advancement.

I can only imagine what Paul might have been feeling at the moment. Everyone who once stood by him has now deserted him at his moment of need. Only Luke remained. Left alone with his thoughts and memories, I'm certain he knew all too well the painful sting of disappointment and the loss with which he was now left. With subtle sadness and sorrow Paul writes to Timothy, "You are aware of the fact that all who are in Asia turned away from me" (2 Timothy 1:15, NASB).

Paul was not the first to experience this kind of grief. Many saints of God have had to face this fact of life at some point in their journey—we will, even in the ministry, have to suffer loss and disappointment.

From the beginning of time this has been evident. Consider God as one example. Love Himself decided one day to set out on one of His most unique and glorious ideas—the creation of man, someone on whom He could lavish His love and be loved by in return. But in a short time, that communion was interrupted, as the beloved betrayed the Lover and chose to go his own way.

In fact, all throughout the Bible, men of God experienced the piercing pain of loneliness and desertion by those nearest to them. Just think of David. Loneliness seemed to be the backdrop of his life—from first starting out with the lonely profession of a shepherd, to being separated from his dearest friend, Jonathan, to hiding alone in caves to preserve his life from the king who sought to kill him. Then later in his life, his closest friend and advisor, Ahithophel, would desert him, even joining sides with David's son who rebelled against him (see 2 Samuel 15:31). His son, his wife, his friends and even his own countrymen—David knew desertion from them all.

As a leader in God's work, Paul had to face the desertion and loneliness that come with that kind of responsibility. In this, he walked in the footsteps of his Master. During Christ's life on earth, He also experienced this desertion, one time having the majority of his disciples walk away: "From this time many of his disciples turned back and no longer followed him" (John 6:66).

By the very nature and the call of the individual to lead God's work, as a pastor, evangelist or any position of service in the kingdom, there is the aloneness and times of painful loss that will be experienced more than once.

Perhaps you find yourself going through similar situations as these men. Maybe, as I'm sure these men did, you cry out wondering why you have been left alone, why that loved one deserted you, why the one you trusted has hurt you so deeply. Scripture reveals some reasons why, which we will look at now.

Reasons Why

There are many reasons why people leave us, even after being close to us and sharing the same heart. For Demas, Paul's beloved coworker, it was the love of this present world that lured him away and caused him to desert Paul. For Ahithophel, David's friend and closest advisor, it was bitterness that took root in his heart and bore the fruit of revenge, causing him to betray his friend and king. And in the heavens, before time began, God dealt with the first experience of betrayal when Lucifer, the once mighty angel, fell through rebellion. When Lucifer was created, God never intended for His most glorious angel, the leader of the entire angelic realm, to become Satan, the enemy of God Almighty. But God did not want him to be a slave, so He gave Lucifer a free mind and heart—the freedom to choose—and the outcome has been evident ever since.

God has given each one of His servants this same freedom to choose. That is why these same scenarios continue to happen all around us today. On and on, this disappointment occurs in the life of servants of God, wounding with the sting of betrayal and causing us to wonder why.

I, too, have dealt with this in our own movement. There was a time when the Lord led me to speak a very strong message to the families on staff at our U.S. office. Because of it, a good number of these brothers and sisters left the ministry in just a matter of weeks. It hurt to see them go. We had labored together for the sake of the unreached. Yet despite the questions and pain of loss, I knew the Lord wanted me to say what I said and deep within my heart knew that He had a purpose in allowing this to happen.

Only time would tell what those purposes would be. And indeed, they were revealed. The following year the organization grew a hundred percent without even adding one more staff member! We had only so many people, yet no work was left undone. We were able to do everything and much more. It was a marvelous time of growth together as we trusted the Lord.

You see, at times the Lord allows these losses to teach us as well as to bring cleansing. Can you imagine if God had not cleansed heaven of the rebellion in Lucifer's heart? Or think about Moses and the incident of rebellion that he faced with Korah (see Numbers 16). We must understand that sometimes God brings about a cleansing process so that He can rebuild and strengthen individual lives and movements. Many ministries can testify to this same type of experience. At the time it may be painful, yet in the end the hand of God was at work all along.

However, this does not mean that everyone who leaves you or the ministry automatically falls under this reason. As I look back over more than 30 years of ministry and leadership within this movement, I must tell you that there are people who are not part of us today who should be here. I cannot just say, "God cleansed the organization and now we are holy and growing." That has not always been true. Through my own emotional outbursts, through gossip I failed to check out or through wrong conclusions I made without full understanding, I have been responsible for people leaving. It was not because God cleansed them out or because they were evil people. It was because I caused them to go. I should have been patient, forgiving and gentle, seeing beyond their mistakes, failures, temperaments and discouragements. I should have been more sensitive and gracious with them and given them second, third or fourth chances, just as God has often given me. But I did not.

I praise God though for the lessons He taught me through my own failure and for forgiving me and helping me lead with more grace and love.

Whatever the reason may be, whether it's bitterness or rebellion, God's cleansing or our own fault, this fact of life remains— we will suffer loss and disappointment in the ministry.

Look at the lives of men and women throughout the Bible. Study the lives of those servants who have gone before you. In each you will find this to be true. And this consistency in the lives of so many servants of God leaves us only to simply accept it as part of the fabric of our lives. And in accepting this kind of suffering, trust God. For peace never comes through answers; peace comes through trust. Peace comes through knowing the One who calls you by name, knowing that He is good and perfect in all His ways and that He cares deeply and tenderly for each of His children, for you. Paul trusted not in answers, but the Answer—his Faithful Father, his Good Shepherd, his Sovereign Lord.

My brother or sister, maybe a dear coworker has left you,

maybe your spouse, either physically or emotionally, is absent, perhaps a child has turned his back on you, or a fellow worker in the ministry left because of a better, higher-paying job. Whoever the person may be and for whatever reason, this element is simply a fact of life—we will be left on our own at times. We will be the one who is left holding the loneliness. But we need not stay there. For the God who allows disappointment and desertion is also the God of all comfort, being our constant companion and bringing encouragement through brothers and sisters who remain until the end.

A Constant Companion

The loss Paul dealt with did not end in hopelessness. In the midst of it all, he recognized that he always had a faithful, constant companion.

> But the Lord stood at my side and gave me strength, so that through me the message might be fully proclaimed and all the Gentiles might hear it. And I was delivered from the lion's mouth. The Lord will rescue me from every evil attack and will bring me safely to his heavenly kingdom. To him be glory for ever and ever (2 Timothy 4:17–18).

In the Lord's company, Paul found his strength. You see, even when our dearest loved ones and coworkers may leave us, the Lord will stand by our side and give us strength, just as Paul experienced. In a moment of great anguish within his soul, Paul found the Lord to be near. Truly, He is a sure refuge and a strong tower (see Psalm 9:9; 61:3) and "an ever-present help in trouble" (Psalm 46:1).

Just as Paul faced many trials in the work of the Lord, and

just as you and I will, God still makes sure we are not alone. Further on in 2 Timothy 4, we find Paul no longer listing the names of those who left him, but rather those people who stood by his side—faithful, godly coworkers, prayer partners and faithful team members who love him and have remained with him.

Luke is one of those people. Known to have been converted by Paul during his missionary journey to Troas, this Gentile and doctor became the companion of Paul, first following him into Philippi and joining with him again at different stages of Paul's ministry. It was in Paul's last days that the "beloved physician" stayed by his side until the very end.

My brother or sister, there will always be a Luke in your life; there will always be a Timothy; there will always be a Tychicus; there will always be a Philemon; there will always be an Aquila and Priscilla; and there will always be a Claudia—a household, a person that stands beside you, even the Lord Himself.

Let us then lift up our eyes to our Sovereign God who has compassion for His servants and cast every one of our cares upon Him. Because as long as we live in this fallen world with fallen humanity, we will deal with the pain of loss. But when it comes, how I pray that each of us would respond like Paul, lifting our eyes and trusting our God, and finding Him faithfully standing at our side, giving us the strength to continue to run the race set before us until the very end.

He is with you always.

twenty

leaving a legacy

Grace. Paul's journey began in grace, and now, as he finishes his last words to Timothy, it ends with grace. *The Lord be with your spirit, Timothy. Grace be with you.*

Grace. God gives grace to the humble, to the weak and to the helpless. These were the words Paul had to offer Timothy before turning his face and traveling the three miles to the chopping block, where the sword would come down in full force to sever his head.

As I read this, I can't help but wonder at the intense emotion of these final moments. I suspect that Luke, his companion and personal physician, with tears, pleaded to the prison guards to let him stay with Paul until the act was done. But they would not. Alone, he would have to wait in the distance and watch his friend go on his own. But Paul was not really alone. The Lord was with his spirit. Grace was with him. And as he had known so intimately along every leg of his journeys, grace would sustain him until finally, it brought him safely home.

Numerous words that Paul spoke to the different churches seem to rush back into my mind as I think of this man of God soon approaching his death. One in particular, written just a few years prior to the believers in Philippi—"I eagerly expect and hope that I will in no way be ashamed, but will have sufficient courage so that now as always Christ will be exalted in my body, whether by life or by death. For to me, to live is Christ and to die is gain" (Philippians 1:20–21). Sufficient courage was his, along with sufficient grace. He had glorified his God in his body, and now he would do so in his death.

I can only imagine the words, thoughts, faces and every hopeful promise that flooded his heart and mind as he made his way to the execution block. This murderer turned father of the faith was soon going to see the face of the One who met him on the Damascus road; the One whose words and light penetrated through his callous, blind heart and brought him life; the One who stood by his side on stormy seas and empowered him with the grace to keep pressing forward. And here he is. The race has been run. The finish line is in sight.

And, as any exuberant runner, when the finish line is in sight, the step is not slowed. No. A sprint begins that propels even the tired and weary forward in hope and excitement, knowing victory awaits, knowing rest awaits. This was Paul. Although he could see the axe in the hand of his executioners, he knew it was not death that lay before him, but life, true and everlasting. Maybe his heart pounded within his chest, not with fear but with a steady anticipation, a joy, knowing he was nearing home. He had fought the good fight. And as he had just finished writing to his son, Timothy, not too long ago, "There is in store for me the crown of righteousness, which the Lord, the righteous Judge, will award to me on that day" (2 Timothy 4:8).

These final scenes roll in slow motion within me: The aged mentor is stripped and forced down on his knees before the cold, stone pillar. In the gentle light of dawn, his back and neck are exposed to the dull blade of this axe that has brought the death of many a criminal in Rome. But before the axe completes its purpose, his body is beaten with rods one last time. I can't help but pause and think back to all his journeys, times when he was beaten mercilessly in one town after the next. The same salty taste of blood in his mouth, the same aching swell, the same sting as his body is torn open with each blow. But this time it is different. It's the last and final. And as with all the others, if not more, it is worth it. He who called him has been faithful. This is grace bringing him home.

Then the moment came. Paul's head was severed from his beaten body. His spirit soared into the heavens to be embraced by everlasting arms. He had kept the faith.

I imagine Luke walked toward his dear friend and, weeping, fell over his lifeless body. *Paul, you made it. Though I may be left alone now, I thank you for the life and the model you gave me. I may not be killed as you were, but however it comes, I can't wait to see you again. We will talk about the rest of the story when I get there.* He then scooped the body up in his arms and carried it away, along with the severed head, to give it a clean, godly burial.

As for Timothy, I doubt he stopped crying for days. I wonder if Luke took this young man, embraced him and consoled him, saying, *Son, I'm an old man like our friend Paul, but you are young. Do you remember the last thing your father told you? He said, "Grace be with you."* In the midst of bearing great sorrow, Timothy also had great responsibility now upon his shoulders. It was grace that carried Paul through, and it was grace that Paul left with Timothy. It was not rules, regulations, knowledge, ability or connections that would sustain, but grace. *My son, legalism, bondage, scolding and fighting won't carry you through. No, it's grace, Timothy. Grace. That's all you need. Now let's go and continue the journey.*

My brothers and sisters, today you and I continue to learn from Paul and Timothy, though they are long gone. Similar to their time and task, a great challenge lies before us as well, a challenge for a time such as this. As a brother I encourage you—as you work on your mission field in Myanmar, Nepal, Sri Lanka, Bangladesh, Bhutan, Sikkim and all over India—not to worry about your imperfections or failures. Don't worry about the past. Don't worry about friends or enemies. And don't worry about your inabilities, youthfulness, fragile body or family struggles. All these problems are part of life. They are the reason God gave us our example in Timothy.

Go on with the Lord. We have a lot to do. We run a race and have a long way yet to the finish. Please don't let yourself or others quit the race. The burden is great, but the way is clear. Our instructions are complete. His grace is sufficient.

May the Lord bless you, strengthen you, encourage you and cover you with His grace. Until we meet in heaven, may God continue to show us His grace and mercy. When it is all said and done, let us be people who say, "Grace, grace, grace." Amen.

Press on against the wind.

notes

Chapter 1: A Higher Call

1. A.W. Tozer, *Gems of Tozer* (Camp Hill, PA: Christian Publications, 1969), p. 89.
2. *Ibid.*, pp. 46–47.
3. John R.W. Stott, *Guard the Gospel* (Downers Grove, IL: Inter-Varsity Press, 1973), p. 49.

Chapter 2: Called by God

1. Author Unknown
2. J. Oswald Sanders, *Spiritual Leadership* (Chicago, IL: Moody Press, 1986), p. 39.

Chapter 3: Life of Integrity

1. *Webster's New Collegiate Dictionary,* 3rd ed. (New York, NY: Simon and Schuster, 1997).
2. Definition taken from http://www.hyperdictionary.com/dictionary/sincere.

Chapter 4: By His Spirit

1. Zac Poonen, *Beauty for Ashes* (Katunayake, Sri Lanka: New Life Literature, 1973), pp. 72–73.

Chapter 5: Living by Self-Discipline

1. J. Oswald Sanders, *Spiritual Leadership,* p. 67.
2. Christina Rossetti, *The Complete Poems,* ed. R.W. Crump (London: Penguin Books LTD, 2001), p. 219.

Chapter 6: Courageous in Battle

1. "June 8, 1978 • Solzhenitsyn's Commencement Speech," Christian History Institute (http://www.gospelcom.net/chi/DAILYF/2001/06/daily-06-08-2001.shtml).
2. *The American Heritage Dictionary of the English Language,* 4th ed. (Boston, MA: Houghton Mifflin Company, 2000).

Chapter 8: Disciple Maker

1. Dr. Robert E. Coleman, *The Master Plan of Evangelism* (Grand Rapids, MI: Revell Publishers, 1993), pp. 58–59.

Chapter 9: Willing to Suffer for His Sake

1. Watchman Nee, *The Character of God's Workman* (New York, NY: Christian Fellowship Publishers, Inc., 1988), p. 39.
2. *Ibid.,* p. 37.
3. *Ibid.,* p. 44.
4. Taken from *Mountain Breezes* by Amy Carmichael. Copyright © 1999 The Dohnavur Fellowship. Published by CLC Publications, Fort Washington, PA. Used by permission.

Chapter 12: Being a Man of the Word

1. Al Maxey, "Cutting Straight the Word," *Grace Centered Magazine* (http://www.gcmagazine.net/cuttingstraight.html).
2. *WordNet* ® 2.0, © 2003, Princeton University (http://dictionary.reference.com/search?r=2&q=commitment).

Chapter 13: Set Apart to Walk in Holiness

1. Zac Poonen, "Living as Jesus Lived," Christian Fellowship Centre, Bangalore (www.cfcindia.com/cda/books/ebooks/Living_as_Jesus_Lived.pdf).
2. Zac Poonen, *Needed: Men of God* (Bombay, India: Gospel Literature Service, 1971), pp. 14–15.

3. Charles R. Swindoll, *The Tale of the Tardy Oxcart* (Nashville, TN: W Publishing Group, 1998), p. 565.

Chapter 15: Man of Discernment

1. *Webster's Revised Unabridged Dictionary* (Plainfield, NJ: MICRA, Inc., 1998).
2. Based on notes taken from Zac Poonen's teaching, spoken at the Asian Biblical Seminary in 2002.

Chapter 18: Determined to Finish

1. Charles R. Swindoll, *The Tale of the Tardy Oxcart,* p. 441.

If this book has been a blessing to you, please
send us a letter in care of the address below.
Thank you.

GFA Books
1800 Golden Trail Court
Carrollton, TX 75010

BOOKS
a division of Gospel for Asia
www.gfa.org

 GOSPEL FOR ASIA

After 2,000 years of Christianity, how can it be that nearly 3 billion people are still unreached with the Gospel? How long must they wait?

This is why Gospel for Asia exists.

More than 20 years ago, God specifically called us to invest our lives to reach the most unreached of the Indian subcontinent through training and sending out native missionaries.

Gospel for Asia (GFA) is a church-planting organization dedicated to reaching the most unreached in the 10/40 Window. Our 14,500 pastors and missionaries serve full-time to plant churches in India, Nepal, China, Bhutan, Myanmar, Sri Lanka, Bangladesh, Laos, Vietnam and Thailand.

Native missionaries are highly effective because they work in their own or a similar culture. They already know, or can easily learn, the language, customs and culture of the people to whom they minister. They don't need visas, and they live economically at the same level as their neighbors. These advantages make them one of the fastest and most effective ways to get the Gospel to the millions who are still waiting to be reached. By God's grace, GFA missionaries have established more than 21,000 churches and mission stations in the past 10 years.*

However, the young, economically weak Asian Church and her missionaries can't do it alone. The enormous task of evangelizing nearly 3 billion people takes the help of the whole Body of Christ worldwide.

That is why GFA offers those who cannot go themselves the opportunity to become senders and prayer partners of native missionaries—together fulfilling the Great Commission and sharing in the eternal harvest of souls.

To find out more information about Gospel for Asia or to receive a free copy of K.P. Yohannan's best-selling book *Revolution in World Missions*, visit our website at www.gfa.org or contact one of our offices near you.

* As of 2004

UNITED STATES 1800 Golden Trail Court, Carrollton, TX 75010
      Toll free: 1-800-946-2742   Email: info@gfa.org

AUSTRALIA P.O. Box 3587, Village Fair, Toowoomba QLD 4350
      Phone: (07) 4630-1580   Email: infoaust@gfa.org

CANADA 245 King Street E, Stoney Creek, ON L8G 1L9
      Toll free: 1-888-WIN-ASIA   Email: infocanada@gfa.org

GERMANY Postfach 13 60, 79603 Rheinfelden (Baden)
      Phone: 7623 797477   Email: infogermany@gfa.org

NEW ZEALAND P.O. Box 302-580, North Harbour, Auckland 1330
      Toll free: 0508-918-918   Email: infonz@gfa.org

SOUTH AFRICA P.O. Box 28880, Sunridge Park, Port Elizabeth 6008
      Phone: 041 360-0198   Email: infoza@gfa.org

UNITED KINGDOM FREEPOST NAT11108, PO BOX 166 YORK YO10 5ZY
      Freephone: 0800 083 9277   Email: infouk@gfa.org

A higher standard.
A higher purpose.

OTHER BOOKS
BY K.P. YOHANNAN

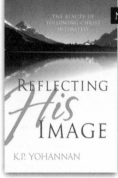

REFLECTING HIS IMAGE

K.P. Yohannan takes us on a journey back to God's original purpose for each of our lives: to reflect His image. This book is a compilation of short, easy-to-read chapters that deal with following Christ closely.

Order ISBN: 1-59589-005-X

THE ROAD TO REALITY

K.P. Yohannan gives an uncompromising call to live a life of simplicity to fulfill the Great Commission.

Order ISBN: 1-59589-002-5

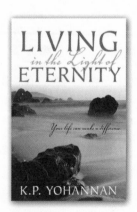

LIVING IN THE LIGHT OF ETERNITY

K.P. Yohannan lovingly, yet candidly, reminds Christians of their primary role while here on earth: harvesting souls. This book challenges us to look at our heart attitudes, motivation and our impact on eternity.

Order ISBN: 1-59589-004-1

For more information on Gospel for Asia, visit *www.gfa.org*

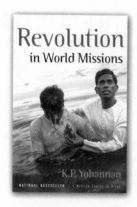

REVOLUTION IN WORLD MISSIONS

In this exciting and fast-moving narrative, K.P. Yohannan shares how God brought him from his remote jungle village to become the founder of Gospel for Asia.

Order ISBN: 1-59589-001-7

COME, LET'S REACH THE WORLD

How effective are the Church's current missions strategies? Are the unreached hearing the Gospel? K.P. Yohannan examines the traditional approach to missions—its underlying assumptions, history and fruit—in light of Scripture and the changing world scene. This book is a strong plea for the Body of Christ to partner with indigenous missionaries so that the whole world may hear.

Order ISBN: 1-59589-003-3

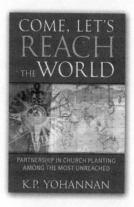

For more information on Gospel for Asia, visit *www.gfa.org*

EXCITING DVDs

THE CALL TO HARVEST

In this 25-minute DVD, you'll meet the people who are near to the Father's heart: the unreached. See them through the eyes of native missionaries like Titus and Joseph, who face danger and hardship to preach the Gospel in Asia. As the life-giving presence of Jesus transforms lives and families daily, the Lord is calling His people everywhere to come and share the joy of this harvest.

Order ISBN: 1-59589-009-2

CHRIST'S CALL: "FOLLOW MY FOOTSTEPS"

In this compelling 41-minute DVD, K.P. Yohannan challenges us to follow in Christ's footsteps—steps that will deliver us from our self-centeredness and cause us to impact the lost millions in our generation.

Order ISBN: 1-59589-006-8

TO LIVE IS CHRIST!

Feel the passion of K.P. Yohannan as he describes the life-giving power of total commitment to Christ in this 55-minute DVD. Be amazed by stories of missionaries who risk their lives to preach the Gospel. Weep with him as he recalls his mother's years of sacrifice that changed lives for eternity. Many people search in vain for the path that leads to the abundant life that Jesus promised. K.P., through the Word of God, uncovers that path in this inspiring and challenging message.

Order ISBN: 1-59589-007-6

For more information on Gospel for Asia, visit *www.gfa.org*

JOURNEY WITH JESUS SERIES

VOLUME ONE

Living by Faith, Not By Sight (56 pp); **Journey with Jesus** (56 pp);
That They All May Be One (56 pp); **Principles in Maintaining a Godly
Organization** (48 pp)

Order ISBN: 1-59589-032-7

VOLUME TWO

A Life of Balance (80 pp); **The Way of True Blessing** (56 pp);
Seeing Him (48 pp); **Dependence Upon the Lord** (48 pp)

Order ISBN: 1-59589-033-5

VOLUME THREE

The Lord's Work Done in the Lord's Way (72 pp); **The Beauty of
Christ through Brokenness** (72 pp); **Learning to Pray** (64 pp);
Stay Encouraged (56 pp)

Order ISBN: 1-59589-034-3

For more information on Gospel for Asia, visit *www.gfa.org*

FREE EMAIL UPDATES
Sign up today at www.gfa.org

Hear from today's heroes of the mission field.

Have their stories and prayer requests sent straight to your inbox.

- ▶ **Fuel your prayer life with compelling news and photos from the mission field.**

- ▶ **Stay informed with links to important video and audio clips.**

- ▶ **Learn about the latest opportunities to reach the lost world.**

GFA sends updates every two weeks. You may cancel your free subscription at any time. We will not sell or release your email address for any reason.

SEND

A NATIVE MISSIONARY TODAY!

I want to help native missionaries reach their own people for Jesus.

I understand that it takes from $90–$180† a month to fully support a native missionary, including family support and ministry expenses.

TO BEGIN SPONSORING TODAY,

visit our website at www.gfa.org

or call us in the US at 1-800-WIN-ASIA (1-800-946-2742)
Phone numbers for other national offices are listed on page 225.

or fill out the form below and mail to the nearest GFA office.
National office addresses are listed on the order form on page 225.

❏ Starting now, I will prayerfully help support _____ native missionary(ies) at $30†† each per month = $_____ a month.

You'll receive a photo and testimony of each native missionary you help sponsor.

❏ Please send me more information about how to help sponsor a native missionary, including a one-year FREE subscription to *SEND!*—"The Voice of Native Missions."

Please circle: Mr. Mrs. Miss Rev.

Name _____

Address _____

City _____ State/PR/County _____ Zip/PC _____

Country _____ Phone (_____) _____

Email _____

❏ Please send me free email updates.

HA62-RB6S   DO62-RB6S   ZHW2-RB6S   3HW2-RB6S   YHW2-RB6S

CHARTER **ECFA** MEMBER

A higher standard.
A higher purpose.

Gospel for Asia sends 100 percent of your missionary support to the mission field. Nothing is taken out for administrative expenses. All donations are tax deductible as allowed by law.

† AUS $120–$200, CAN $90–$180, €45–60, CHF80–110, NZ $140–$240, UK £60–£100, ZA R540–R900.

†† AUS $40, CAN $30, €30, CHF60, NZ $40, UK £20, ZA R150.

FREE subscription

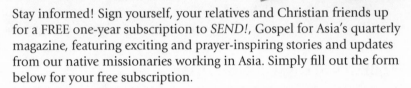

FOR YOU AND YOUR FRIENDS

Stay informed! Sign yourself, your relatives and Christian friends up for a FREE one-year subscription to *SEND!*, Gospel for Asia's quarterly magazine, featuring exciting and prayer-inspiring stories and updates from our native missionaries working in Asia. Simply fill out the form below for your free subscription.

Please circle: Mr. Mrs. Miss Rev.

Name _____

Address _____

City _____ State/PR/County _____ Zip/PC _____

Country _____ Phone (____) _____

Email _____

❑ Please send me free email updates

Please circle: Mr. Mrs. Miss Rev.

Name _____

Address _____

City _____ State/PR/County _____ Zip/PC _____

Country _____ Phone (____) _____

Email _____

❑ Please send me free email updates

HA62-PB6G   DO62-PB6G   ZHW2-PB6G   3HW2-PB6G   YHW2-PB6G

Include additional names on a separate sheet of paper.

❑ Please identify me as the gift subscription donor.

My name is: _____

MAIL THIS FORM to one of Gospel for Asia's national offices listed on page 225.